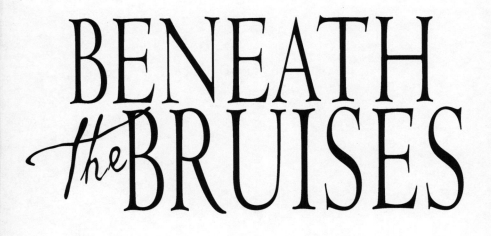

BENEATH *the* BRUISES

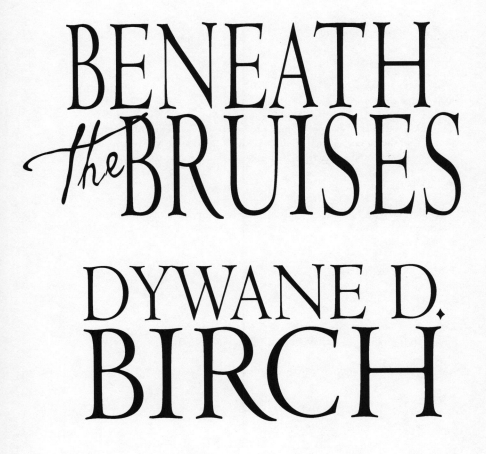

BENEATH *the* BRUISES

DYWANE D. BIRCH

SBI

STREBOR BOOKS

NEW YORK LONDON TORONTO SYDNEY

Strebor Books
P.O. Box 6505
Largo, MD 20792
http://www.streborbooks.com

ISBN-13 978-1-59309-208-5

LCCN 2008935885

Cover design: © www.mariondesigns.com
Cover photograph: © Keith Saunders/Marion Designs

First Strebor Books trade paperback edition November 2008

10 9 8 7 6 5 4 3 2 1

Manufactured in the United States of America

For information regarding special discounts for bulk purchases,
please contact Simon & Schuster Special Sales at 1-800-456-6798
or business@simonandschuster.com

DEDICATION

This book is dedicated to my sister Melissa,
and the countless number of women
who have loved more than they have loved themselves;
who continue to love, hoping, wishing, praying
for someone to love them back.
Love is not abuse...
Reclaim your hearts
Redirect your destinies
Spread your wings
And fly.

You are beautiful.
You are worthy.
You are love.

ACKNOWLEDGMENTS

All praises to the One who continues to order my steps. I am truly blessed!

To my family for always loving me no matter the distance between us; you all hold very special places in my heart.

To my wonderful friends (you know who you are) for the love, laughter and beautiful memories. I am forever grateful!

To Sara Camilli, my agent, for always being supportive and encouraging. I can't thank you enough. All that you do is… Priceless!

To Zane for her undying support of (and belief in) my literary endeavors; you continue to inspire me. Charmaine Parker, thank you, thank you, thank you! I appreciate you more than you'll ever know. To the rest of the Strebor staff: thanks for all that you have done, and all that you will continue to do; and, last but not least—a special thanks to my publicist Yona Deshommes for being…you!

To all the Strebor authors, it's a blessing to be amongst such great talent. I wish you all continued success in all of your literary endeavors. Keep the pens flowing, my literary brothers and sisters!

To my "special" author friends, the ones I vibe with on a regular: Allison Hobbs (love you, freaky baby!), Anna J (uh, you already know what it is. After giving me twenty-one babies, you will always be my number one "baby momma"—no matter who else I give my love to), Danita Carter (I'm so proud of you. We gotta hook up, soon, to celebrate!), Tu-Shonda Whitaker (Thanks for always sharing ideas, and being able to keep it real. I love your energy. I'm so glad we connected!), and Collen Dixon (I love you!).

To Nakea Murray (the Wop queen) for always encouraging and challenging me to step outside the box. Thank you for being you! You're doin' big things so keep shakin' the haters off ya.

To Angela Coleman, Derek Overton, Cashana Seals (and the rest of the Imani Book Club sistas), Tiffany Colvin and countless others: Thank you for continuing to ride this literary wave with me. I truly appreciate the camaraderie, and your loyal support.

To all the wonderful readers (and book clubs) who continue to support my literary endeavors. From my soul to yours… I thank you from the bottom of my heart. Without you, this fascinating journey would not be possible. I am forever grateful to you!

Soulfully,

Dywane
email: bshatteredsouls@cs.com
www.myspace.com/dywaneb

PREFACE

As an optimistic romantic at heart, I'll be the first to admit that I believe in romance and the power of love. That I believe in miracles, and that dreams do come true. I believe we all have soul mates, and that there are reasons why people enter our lives, and why we choose to allow them to stay. No matter the purpose, no matter the outcome, there are always some very valuable lessons to be learned about life and love and who we are as individuals.

I am also a realist. I know that love and relationships go through stages. That people outgrow each other and that relationships oftentimes dissolve. That there will always be bumps along the way in every relationship, and conflicts may arise. That people will not always be honest, nor will their intentions always be good. And we will be faced with disappointments and disillusionments at some point in our lives. Still, there is no reason for disrespect. No excuse for violence. Abuse is a choice. It does not happen by chance. It is a pattern of behavior. It begins with a thought. It is reinforced by a belief. And it continues as a cycle. To break its destructive, never-ending spin we have to somehow discover new and better ways of loving each other, communicating with each other, and expressing ourselves without disrespect and the use of violence. We have to find the strength to no longer remain in unhealthy and unsafe situations; to be able to recognize when a relationship has run its course and let go without malice or resentment. How wonderful the world would be if life were that simple.

Disturbingly, in a climate where silence is a batterer's best friend and domestic violence continues to climb to epidemic proportions, someone, somewhere, is being beaten about the face and body. Someone's screams go unheard. Someone's tears fall unchecked. Someone's bruises go unnoticed. Someone's home is being turned into a battlefield. And—without remorse, without regard—another life is taken.

Although this is a work of fiction, its content is real. Its message is clear. This is not about anger management. Abuse never is. It is about power and control. It is about choices. It is more than just a story conjured up in the creative mind of a man who knows nothing about violence. On the contrary, I know all too well the devastating effects it has on a family. I have lived in it. I have seen it. I have heard it. I have felt it. And I have done my best to avoid it.

Over the last three years, I have worked with the offenders of domestic violence, and I have heard their stories, abridged and unabridged versions, some as real and as painfully raw as they can get. Others were fluffed with minimizations, justifications, and rationalizations as to why the offenders do what they do. Many have expressed remorse and deep desires to change. Others take no responsibility and, unfortunately, make no real investments in themselves or in their families to become better men, husbands or fathers. Sadly, they will continue to be who they are. That is the reality. There will be (and are) countless numbers of women who stay, hoping, wishing, praying for a change that may never come. Still, they remain, desperately trying to be all that he wants, expects, and demands her to be. This too is a reality. There is no judgment being made, just a statement of facts. They will continue to love their men, the fathers of their children, no matter what. They will sacrifice themselves for the sake of holding on to a marriage or a relationship that is controlling, degrading, and disrespectful. They will blame themselves and make excuses for the abuse. No matter how much they may want to, in their hearts and minds, leaving is not always a viable option for them.

In writing this book, I recognize that I have only scratched and banged at the surface. Still I attempt to paint over the dings with quick strokes of a beautifully wrapped, happily-ever-after tale, knowing that this isn't everyone's story; completely understanding that it isn't indicative of everyone's painful journey. There are hundreds of thousands of real-life stories with a multitude of mangled beginnings, middles and endings that are not happy. Where there are no escapes, or at least none without dire, often times deadly, consequences. However, whether there are changes or not; whether the victimized partner stays or leaves, all abusers need to be held accountable. They need to be confronted. They need to be challenged. They need to be held legally responsible for their actions, and they need to be offered the tools and the opportunity to change in a setting specifically geared toward batterer's intervention.

Being the optimist that I am, I believe that all batterers/abusers (men and women) can change if they choose to, if they have the overwhelming desire to. Despite distorted belief systems about what relationships are and aren't, despite negative-thinking patterns, despite sometimes unrealistic perceptions of what domestic violence is or isn't, I believe in the power of change. For now, I will remain in the trenches addressing and confronting and challenging. And I, too, will continue to hope and pray and wish for peace, love, and happy endings.

Beneath the Bruises evolved out of a poem I wrote over three years ago. It is dedicated to every woman who has ever been exposed to violence. It is my testament to those who were able to leave, and for those who have chosen to stay (no matter what their reasons). It is my tribute to those who lost their lives in the struggle. It is my celebration of women and their strengths to endure, to overcome, and to continuously rise. You are beautiful. You are worthy. You are love. You are survivors. It is my sincerest hope that this book, my humble offering to you, becomes someone's source of strength, that it becomes a beacon of light that safely guides someone toward their own march to mental, emotional, physical, and spiritual freedom. That it brings them comfort knowing that they are not alone; that it is not their fault; that this too shall pass.

One

I am a wife. I am a mother. I am a woman. But I am not my own person. I am someone I do not know—someone I care not to be. Consequently, I have become the face of many facades. Sadly, no one knows this. They do not know that behind the smiles that have become plastered formality, there is a river of tears that I keep hidden, and my life—with all of its makings of success—has become beautifully deceptive.

Elusive images of what my life is, and is not, dangle from the enormous bay window of my sixty-five-hundred-square-foot home—with its inlaid marble floors and vaulted cathedral ceilings nestled within a well-heeled and well-educated community. From the outside, you'd think I had the perfect life, and on the surface I do. I'm married to my high school sweetheart, a successful investment banker three years my senior—a summa cum laude graduate of Morehouse College and Pace University with master's degrees in finance and economics. He is a well-respected, shrewd businessman who has strategically and methodically amassed more money than he'll ever spend in this lifetime. I have watched my husband climb the ladder of accomplishment, watched him become the man that he is, and I have reaped the rewards and the consequences of it.

In the early stages of our relationship, he swept me off my feet with his intense eyes, mischievous grin, seductive physical presence, and charming demeanor. It was his confidence mixed with a hint of arrogance that intrigued me and intensified my desires to be with him. Truth be told, he was my first and only. My first boyfriend, my first kiss, and my first love. So it was only natural that he'd become my husband and the father of my children. I knew it was my destiny the moment I laid eyes on him on the basketball court in my freshman year. He was poster-boy handsome, academically gifted, and blessed with an effortless athletic ability that left everyone in awe. Teachers, coaches, parents, and peers—both male and female—cheered for him, especially me, who fell head over heels in love with him. I knew, along with everyone else who adored him, that he was destined for greatness.

I can still remember the night before he went off to college on a scholarship, how he had carved our initials into a sturdy oak tree in his backyard, stating our love would always stay rooted and weather any storm. I stared into his dark chocolate eyes and soaked in the richness of his voice telling me how much I meant to him, drinking in his promises of a wonderful life together. He vowed to love me, protect me, and take care of me 'til death did us part. Then he pressed his lips against mine and caused waves of bliss to ripple through me. When he stepped back from me, he took my face into his big, warm hands and softly said, "You're mine now. Don't ever forget that, you hear me?" I nodded, gazing into his eyes as tears filled mine. "Promise me you won't let anyone else have your love." Without hesitation, I promised. Right then, I signed over my heart to him. He wiped my tears as they slowly fell, and planted gentle kisses all over my face. He said I held the key to his heart. And I believed him. I knew then I could never give myself to anyone else. I knew no one else would ever make me feel the way he did. And I kept my promise. I saved myself for the only man I knew I would ever love.

Three years later, I went off to Spelman and fell in love with him all over again, embracing my future. I had so many dreams. I would pledge, like my sister had before me. Would join organizations. Pursue a career and become a successful journalist or doctor. Then something within me changed. As if on cue, my husband's visions quickly became mine. Pledging a sorority or becoming active in other campus groups became forbidden thoughts. He didn't want those things to interfere with our ability to spend time together. Then, in my junior year, I got pregnant. Slowly, all of my aspirations withered away. Suddenly my life took on a new meaning. Brick by brick, Syreeta Colette Lynch was dismantled, and Mrs. Randall Michael Taylor III was erected.

My plans, everything I wanted, everything I aspired to be, became insignificant. Randy's thoughts became mine. His dreams became mine. My existence became intertwined with his. His happiness became my responsibility. My happiness became contingent on his. My life became dependent on him. He became the air that I breathed, and the beat of my heart.

Now, eleven years and five children later, I'm a thirty-two-year-old housewife and mother with no life outside the one created within the confines of our million-dollar home in the suburbs of Jersey. A world neatly woven together with two luxury cars, an SUV, a minivan, properties in the Hamptons, South Beach and on Martha's Vineyard—along with access to shopping sprees for myself and our children—with his approval, of course. Actually, everything I do must be agreed upon by Randy. If he says no, then he expects me to abide by his decision, and questioning him is definitely not an option. Most of the time, being the obedient wife, I honor his wishes. But on occasion, I speak up—or as he says, challenge him—and it somehow escalates into an argument that lasts for hours, sometimes days, or ends with him saying nothing at all. His silence, his acting as if I'm invisible, hurts more than his words.

Anyway, I'm sure my husband enjoys this reality, the fact that I have to ask his permission before I can spend any of his money. And I'm even more convinced he loves the fact that he doesn't have to compete for my attention with a career, a hobby, or close friends—things that would have given me my own identity.

At five feet nine, 132 pounds, my slanted gray eyes, thick light-brown hair, and flawless cinnamon-colored skin give me what some would say is an exotic look. I have often been mistaken for a model. Some say I favor Stacy Dash. And under different circumstances, I would probably be flattered. However, I don't feel so striking. Not anymore, anyway. Now my looks feel more like a curse, particularly when someone glances at me, or nods, or smiles in my direction. Then I become the one to blame. I have lost count of the number of times that I have been accused of leading men on, flirting with them, teasing them, wanting their attention. Thanks to years of my husband's browbeating, I no longer feel beautiful. No longer feel self-assured. My self-esteem and self-confidence have shriveled to almost nothing.

The tape plays in my head, his voice crisp and callous. "Oh, you like it when some other man is grinning all up in your face, don't you? Makes you feel real special being a dick tease, doesn't it?… You just enjoy disrespecting me, don't you?… Don't get too excited, he doesn't want your fat ass. …I'm the only man who'll ever love you. …You need to watch how much you eat— if I'd wanted a pig, I'd have married one. …You're so stupid." And this is how the song of my current life began. This is how its melody plays. Like a needle stuck in the groove of an old dusty forty-five, his words are scratched in my memory. And no matter how hard I try to replace the sound of his cutting remarks, they still pierce my spirit.

There was a time when I believed I could achieve any- and every thing. But somewhere along my journey through life and love, that part of me evaporated like the droplets of morning dew on blades of grass under a burning sun. Everything I had hoped to be disappeared into thick, stifling air. But I dare not share this with anyone so I go through the motions, make-believing.

Over the years, I have closed my eyes to the images of black eyes and busted lips. I have skillfully learned how to shut off the screaming and yelling in my head, and have moved through life as if I were floating. And it is this facade, the smiles and the glitter—that has been slowly sucking the life out of me. Sorrowfully, my existence is one big lie. And I have to find my escape. But before I can do that, I have to find me: the woman lost in a war zone. The woman who has held on to life, painted by elusive fairy tales and an imaginary happily-ever-after— desperately trying to fix whatever it is I have done wrong. Sadly, I don't know how. And that worries me.

Never in a million years would I, an intelligent, educated

woman, have considered myself being in an abusive relationship. Or identified myself as a victim. How could that be? My
husband adores our children, and me. He's an excellent provider.
And I know in my heart, he would never intentionally do anything to hurt me. Would he? *No*...of course not. He just gets
frustrated—sometimes, and a little cranky when things aren't
to his liking. I can handle his sporadic bouts of abuse. He just
needs to learn ways to deal with his anger. That's all. That's
what I keep telling myself. And that's what I want to believe.
To think otherwise is too painful. It would mean I'd have to
stop looking at my picture-perfect world—the one I've created
in my head and allowed everyone else to see—through rose-
colored lenses. Something in my soul tells me something has
gone terribly awry in my marriage. Nevertheless, I know we
can work this out. At least this is what I hope. My husband is
a good man. And I love him so very much. Like he once said,
we can weather any storm—together. Yet, lately, I feel like I'm
standing in the eye of a tornado, alone.

Two

S o I guess it's the contradictions in my life that compels
me to seek refuge in the comfort of a therapist's office.
It has slowly become my safe haven. A place where I
can cry and peel back layers of myself freely. Without encoun-
tering questioning glances or raised eyebrows, I try to find
myself—wherever she may be. It is the only place where I can
divulge my deepest, darkest secret and not have to feel ashamed
or embarrassed. And it is in the warm, caring eyes of my psych-
ologist that I gradually begin to see myself for the first time,
clearly. The reflection disturbs me. It saddens me to see the
woman I've become. Underneath my expensive makeup and
designer garments I cover up the marks of my life. And it hurts.

I come in before Dr. Curtis and take my usual seat on the
butter-soft brown leather sofa flanked by two oversized chairs.
In front of me is a round marble coffee table. A Maasai sculp-
ture, *Gentle Ruler*, is centered proudly atop it. Large leafy plants
surround the room, while a 150-gallon aquarium filled with
tropical fish adds to the décor. Several canvas oil abstractions
in different shades of oranges, browns, and beiges are on crisp
white walls. In the far left and right corners of the room sit
two enormous vases of exotic flowers on marble pedestals while
sandalwood and patchouli candles in handsome dark wood

candleholders are situated around the room. I breathe in their scent. Inhale. Exhale. Everything about this office is warm and inviting. It's easy to sink, relieved—no matter how briefly—into the overall calmness of the room.

I recall the beginning, long ago and far removed from the first insult hurled like hot lava against my spirit, from the first slap, from the first swollen eye closed by a fist, when my world was being shaped and molded from the clay of my own fantasies.

Before I learned to pretend.

Dr. Curtis smiles at me. "How are you feeling today?"

I shrug my shoulders. "Okay," I reply, feeling his eyes study me.

He leans forward, his hands cupping his chin. His gaze never leaves my face. And I feel myself becoming slowly undone. "Are you sure?"

I nod my head. "Of course," I reply. In the two months I've been coming to see him, it never struck me how handsome he is before now. He has smooth skin the color of honey, long, thick lashes wrapped around hazel eyes. And a captivating smile that lights up the room. I've never noticed his dimpled chin or the deep spin of his short, wavy hair until now. He should be on the cover of a magazine instead of sitting behind a desk, probing minds—my mind. His charming manner and passion for what he does fascinate me, and I wonder what motivates him to sit and listen to the pain of others. My pain. Why is he so devoted to soothing souls? It's a question I want to ask. Perhaps one day I will. For now, he is my only hope that change is going to come.

"Then why don't I believe you?" he responds, leaning back in his high-backed leather chair. He keeps his eyes on me, then adds, "You're shaking your foot, so that tells me there's something going on." I am not aware I am doing this. I stop. Shift in my seat.

He's beginning to know me better than I know myself, which doesn't surprise me. He's an intuitively perceptive man, one who notices and senses everything. I recall the first time I met—I mean, bumped into—him. I was absent-mindedly stepping off the elevator and almost knocked him over. My mind was scrolling fiercely down my "things to do list" before I picked up the children from daycare by three. It was already noon, and I still hadn't made it to Wegman's to pick up dinner or to Rago Brothers in Morristown to drop off my husband's black designer shoes, the ones he desperately needed repaired by Friday to wear with his black pin-striped suit.

"Ooh, excuse me. I'm so sorry," I had said, feeling flustered.

"That's quite all right," the kind voice replied, instinctively reaching out to keep my bags from hitting the floor. "No harm done."

"Thank you," I said, casting my eyes downward behind my sunglasses, feeling suddenly embarrassed by the wide smile that was flashed before me.

"Anytime," he responded, stepping aside. He must have sensed my vulnerability because just as I was walking off, he stopped me, holding open the elevator doors. "Excuse me. I have something for you," he said, reaching into his suit jacket and pulling out a leather billfold. "Here's my card. Just in case you ever find yourself in need of someone to talk to."

I took the cream-colored card, glancing at it. In engraved black script, it read: *Dr. Jordan Curtis, Psy. D. Individual, Group, and Couples' Counseling.*

I gave him a panicked look. *Oh, no. He can see my eye behind these dark glasses*, I thought. "Thanks, but I won't be needing this," I quickly stated.

He smiled again. "I hope not. But hold on to it. Just in case." The elevator doors shut and I was left standing in the middle of the mall, feeling completely exposed. I looked around, wondering if anyone else saw what he had seen—the naked truth.

The last time my husband slapped me, three months ago, was when I decided to pick up the phone and dial Dr. Curtis's number. Randy had questioned me about why it had taken me so long to get back from the grocery store. When I tried to explain that I had run into one of the neighbors and we had become engrossed in conversation about her daughter's upcoming wedding, he insisted I was lying. Even though I had walked into the house with an armload of groceries and had a receipt with the time printed on it to prove my whereabouts, he didn't believe me. The whole ordeal escalated to him accusing me of sneaking off to meet some other man. He yelled and screamed obscenities. Demanded I carry my cell phone anytime I left the house. Threatened to leave me and take the kids away from me if I ever pulled another "stunt" like that again. And before I could get another word in edgewise, before I was able to reassure him, Randy's handprint was on the side of my face. I knew then, I had to do something. Unfortunately, I had cancelled three times before I finally mustered up the nerve to show up.

"I don't really feel like talking about it today, Doc," I say returning my attention to him.

"Okay. So then we sit and say nothing until you're ready. But I'll never be able to help you sort through your emotional turmoil until you start to completely trust me. I am here to help you find the answers you need. I hope you know by now I'm not here to judge you." There is definitely something warm and humble about Dr. Curtis. I am respectfully drawn to him, his energy. The room is filled with his endless concern.

I take in a deep breath and nod. "I do."

He smiles again. "Good. So tell me what's troubling you today, and together we can find a way to work through it."

I inhale, then slowly exhale. "He wants another baby," I blurt, feeling fresh tears rim my eyes. Randy decided three weeks ago that I should get pregnant and "give me a girl this time." That's what he had the nerve to say to me as if I had control over the sex of a child. I was too shocked to respond. Unfortunately, my silence had given him the impression that this is what I want as well, which is so far from the truth. I love my sons dearly, but I am already overwhelmed and can't possibly consider having another baby. Having a ten-year-old, an eight-year-old, and a set of three-year-old triplets is more than enough. Another child would definitely send me over the edge. And, God forbid, if I were to have another son, Randy would make sure I knew it was my fault. That something was wrong with me.

"Is that what you want?"

I shake my head forlornly. "No. Not really."

"What do you mean by 'not really'?"

"I mean I don't want any more kids right now. Five is enough. Wouldn't you say so?" I ask with a slight nervous chuckle.

"That's not for me to decide," he offers. "But... " He opens his arms for me to finish.

"But when I'm pregnant, things between us seem so much better. Randy's much more loving and attentive."

"So you think having another baby is going to keep things that way?"

"I don't know, maybe."

"Are you saying you'd consider getting pregnant just to stop the violence?"

I shake my head. "No, absolutely not," I say. "It's just that I know Randy. And he's insistent on having another baby."

"And he's also very abusive to you," Dr. Curtis states, eyeing me. "Is he not?"

I nod. In my head, I try to recall the number of incidences over the last three years since the birth of the triplets. There were four, the last one being three months ago. "But not all the time," I quickly say.

"Whether it's once a week or once every other year, abuse is still abuse—and it is still a pattern of behavior." He pauses, allows what he has said to settle in, then continues. "Syreeta, pregnancy does not stop domestic violence. Statistics show that one to twenty-five percent of women are battered during their pregnancy."

Suddenly, my mind rolls back to the year 2000, the night the cramping started. The night bolts of pain shot through my stomach, and the flow of warm blood escaped me. I had suffered a miscarriage. It was stress-related. That's what I have allowed myself to accept as truth. It had nothing to do with me trying to get away from Randy during an argument and tripping and falling down the stairs. The heel of my shoe caught in the rug. That's what happened. I'm certain he didn't push me. At least that's what I want to believe. I ignore Dr. Curtis's statement. Neither of us knew I was pregnant, so what he has said doesn't apply to Randy and me. Or does it?

"I just want the fighting to stop," I say.

"Sadly, it won't. In fact, oftentimes the battering increases during this period."

I push back the thoughts, push back the half-truths, cling to my own illusions. "Randy has never hit me while I was pregnant," I say.

"Okay. So the physical abuse stops, but what about the emotional and mental abuse?"

"He just gets a little edgy," I reply defensively.

"Don't make excuses for his behavior. Has he hit you recently?" Dr. Curtis asks, raising his brow. He looks at me intently.

I shake my head. "Not in a while. As long as I don't say or do something he doesn't like, he's the sweetest man."

"So what I hear you saying is that you're responsible for your husband's behaviors, correct?"

"Yes... I mean, no," I say, shifting in my seat.

"Which is it?" he asks.

"No, but..."

"No 'buts,'" he says. "As long as you continue to buy into the belief that somehow you are responsible for how your husband treats you, you will always feel it's your duty to carry and own guilt and blame that do not belong to you."

"I know," I state solemnly. "I'm trying not to. But sometimes it's hard. In my heart, I really believe this time Randy is truly sorry for slapping me, and saying all those nasty things. He really is trying."

"So you're saying everything is going well?"

For now, I think. I want to believe that this reprieve, this peace between Randy and me, is permanent. That the rain and ear-shattering thunder that has kept me drifting, searching for shelter, are finally over and that we can move forward. But there's an aching part of me that defies what's in my heart. I nod. "He's been very attentive, and extremely apologetic."

"Hmm. Sounds like the two of you are in what we call the Honeymoon Stage of the battering cycle. The tension has decreased. He has begged for your forgiveness, and is very loving. You believe everything is better because he has made promises that he will most likely not keep. He's probably showered you with flowers and expensive trinkets to show you just how much you mean to him." I shift in my seat. Dr. Curtis studies me. He peeks into the window of my life. Sees what I try to hide. "Don't be fooled," he says evenly. "It is an illusion. Just like you, he believes it won't happen again. Unfortunately it does, and it will. This stage just reinforces your hope that he will change, that things will be different."

He goes on to explain how tension builds and escalates into violence, and how the pattern is cyclic, and develops in almost two-thirds of many domestic violence relationships. He indicates that the longer the cycle is repeated, the more frequent and severe the violence. I hear what he is saying, but I am struggling to wrap my mind around the possibility that what he says applies to me.

"Unfortunately, denial is what keeps you glued to his abuse," he continues. "Until you're ready to break through it, you will continue to be sucked into this vicious cycle. Nothing changes, if nothing changes. And until your husband is held accountable and takes full responsibility for his behavior, he's going to continue to do what he does."

I raise my eyebrow in surprise. Even though I know what Dr. Curtis says is true, his bluntness catches me off guard. He is usually not so direct. "He doesn't mean it," I respond quickly. I feel the need to defend my husband. "He loves me and would never do anything to hurt me."

"Syreeta, love is not abuse. Your husband's behavior is not about what you say or do. It's about his need to control you. No one should have to live their life walking on eggshells. A batterer batters because he wants to, because it gets him what he wants. Your husband is just that—a batterer. There is no sugarcoating it. Him wanting you to have another baby is just another way for him to keep you under his control."

"I know...but he—"

"What about contraceptives?" he asks, cutting me off. "Have you considered it as a viable way to keep from having another baby until you're ready?"

"Randy would have a fit if I ever suggested such a thing."

He pulls in his lips and nods knowingly. "I'm sure he would. So what other alternatives do you have?"

I squint my eyes, lowering my voice in a conspiratorial whisper. "Doc, you're not suggesting I keep it from him, are you?"

"Not at all. I would never promote secrets. But I do encourage you to find ways to protect yourself. If you aren't ready to have another child, then you need to be able to have some control—or at least, some say—in that."

I sigh heavily. "I'll just have to hope for the best. I'd have hell to pay if I ever brought up the topic of birth control. And God only knows what he'd do if he found out I was taking something to prevent getting pregnant." I think back on the time I wanted to have my tubes tied after giving birth to the triplets, and how Randy refused, stating if I loved him, I wouldn't even consider it. He even went so far as to threaten to leave me and fight for custody of our children if I went through with the procedure. Feeling cornered, I dismissed the idea. And now here we are again, three years later, and he wants another child. What in the world would become of my life if I were to get pregnant?

"So you're saying it's out of your control?"

"I don't know. Maybe."

"Syreeta, you are aware that there are controllable and uncontrollable things in life?"

"Of course."

"So what things in your life do you have the power to control?"

"It's not that simple. Intellectually, I know what I should be able to control. But emotionally…" —I shake my head—"I feel like my life is being orchestrated by a force greater than me."

"No, your life is being *controlled* by someone with his own agenda. That's what happens in domestic violence situations. It distorts what is supposed to be a relationship based on mutual respect for each other's right to say no, and to have their own ideas, feelings, and thoughts. Neither partner has the right to rob the other of that. You are not a puppet, or some mechanical gadget that can be shut on or off."

"That's not what he's doing," I say, lifting my brow.

"Who are you?"

Startled by his question, I tilt my head, then smile nervously. "I don't quite understand the question."

He repeats it.

"Syreeta Taylor," I answer.

"That's the obvious," he states, pressing the tips of his fingers together into a steeple. "But tell me. Who is Syreeta?"

"A wife and mother," I answer.

"Okay, that too is evident. But is that who you *really* are?"

I shrug. "That's all I've become."

"But is that who you always want to be? Is Syreeta happy with being just a wife and mother?"

"Sometimes," I answer, becoming uncomfortable with this line of questioning. My guilt at not being happy with my life has been tearing me apart. It is just too painful to confront. The thought of doing something for myself feels like an act of betrayal against my children, my husband—my family. They depend on me. "What I want or don't want to be isn't important right now."

"Says who? Of course it is. Your perception of who you are, and what you are, greatly influences your decisions. There's nothing wrong with being a good mother and a loving wife, but that is just a small part of who you are, or who you should be. What does Syreeta want for Syreeta?"

I allow the question to slice open my thoughts. An impassive expression finds its way across my face and then my mind drifts, rolling back in time. Four years ago, thanks to my sister's connections, I was offered a position at a major publishing house in New York as an assistant freelance editor. The salary was perfect and the hours were great; I could work from home. I was so thrilled about the offer I was floating, and couldn't wait to share the news with Randy. Unfortunately, I didn't get the reaction I had hoped for. Instead of basking in my enthusiasm, he became argumentative. "What about the kids?" he had asked, scowling.

"I'll be working from home for the most part," I explained.

"I don't think you should stress yourself out about working," he said. "Your attention needs to be focused on taking care of things around here. Something you can barely keep up with."

"Randy, I'll be able to help out financially," I offered, dismissing his snide comment.

"Look around you," he snapped, opening his arms and slowly turning around. "Does it look like we're strapped for cash?"

"No," I admitted. "But it would be nice to have my own money."

"For what? On top of the five hundred dollars a week I give you, I make sure you have everything you need."

"I know, but—"

"What kind of place would be offering *you* employment anyway?" he asked, cutting me off. "You don't know the first thing about editing anything. You've never even had a job."

"But I have the education," I reasoned. I hadn't even accepted the position and he had already questioned my abilities, making me doubt my capabilities. "And it's an entry level position—" I tried to press on, but he shut me down; burst my bubble with tiny pins of insult.

"Big deal," he snorted. "You don't have the skills. You'll end up looking like a big fool when you can't deal with all the pressure of meeting deadlines."

"I know I can—"

"No, I won't allow it," he stated. "Your place is here taking care of our kids. Besides we've already talked about you having another baby. That should be your focus. Not worrying about making a few peanuts." I tried to convince him it would give me something to do until then. That it would allow me some sense of independence. He looked at me as if I had two heads. He became enraged, saying I was disrespecting his role as breadwinner and provider for the family. Said I was being selfish and insensitive. If I really loved him, I'd respect his wishes, and not challenge his authority. I gave up. My mother had instilled in me that a woman's place was beside her husband, supporting his decisions, not questioning them; respecting him as head of household, not undermining him. One month later, I discovered I was pregnant again. And when I learned I was carrying triplets, the thin hope of becoming self-sufficient was sucked into a vacuum and sealed away tight.

I snatch a glance at Dr. Curtis for a moment, then look away. *What does Syreeta want for Syreeta?* There are no answers. I am hurt and there is an aching that forces its way up from the pit of my soul and catches in my throat. I look to Dr. Curtis for the soothing balm needed to heal my wounds. I am feeling robbed of choices, robbed of thoughts. Deprived of the freedom to be me, whoever that is. "I honestly haven't given it any thought," I softly say.

A brief silence comes between us.

"What are some things you're passionate about?" he asks, cutting into the quiet that has crept into the room.

I give him a blank stare. I am expressionless and wordless. I try to construct a string of syllables that make sense. There are none.

Dr. Curtis sees this and tries to help me sort through the expanse of emptiness that has somehow, without warning, become my life. I try to recall exactly how or when I became cocooned into an existence that had nothing to do with me. I try to search for something that I am passionate about. Other than being a good mother and a supportive wife, I have never given any thought to anything else. *Passion*, I repeat in my head. It is a word vaguely familiar yet disturbingly foreign to me, its meaning an anomaly. I struggle desperately to find something that remotely resembles it in my world. Sadly, it is nonexistent in my marriage and in my personal life. Dr. Curtis tells me it does exist, but is buried beneath years of being devalued and denied. He spends the remainder of our session scratching the surface, trying to break through the top layers, trying to uncover what I want for myself. The process is overwhelming. I am slowly becoming exhausted.

"I really don't know," I state. My head starts to pound.

"Then we need to start working on that. Have you given any further thought to group?" He indicates that group is twelve-weeks, psycho-educational, and he tries to convince me how beneficial it would be. He explains how the group is a way for women who are in abusive relationships to come together for information and support and to alleviate the isolation and shame that comes with being victimized. As well as to provide encouragement for women to take initial steps to facilitate their own safety plans.

I shake my head. "I'm not ready for a group," I answer. Individual therapy is safer for me. I don't want to share my pain with a bunch of strangers. Don't want unfamiliar faces and curious eyes peeking into the blisters of my life.

"Being around other women who are experiencing what you're going through would really help empower you, and reinforce that you are not alone in this," he explains, sensing my reservations. The timer on his desk goes off, indicating my session is over. He flips through his planner. "I'm going to schedule you for next Thursday; how is that?"

"Fine," I state, getting up. He gets up as well and extends his hand. My small, manicured hand gets lost in his grip. He shakes it firmly.

"I want you to think long and hard about what it is you want for you, and to really consider group counseling. We'll talk about it next week."

I nod, making my way toward the heavy oak doors after placing a small Band-Aid over a gaping wound I'm afraid will never close on its own.

Three

The clock on my marble vanity reads 9:18 p.m. The kids are fast asleep, and Randy is downstairs in the study doing whatever it is he does when the door is closed. I never have any interest in knowing. I just assume it's work related and I'm okay with that. I walk into my master bathroom and strip naked. My expansive bathroom is where I close myself off to the world. It's where I can steal a few precious moments for myself without hassle. I fill my oversize bathtub with crystals, then pin my hair up. The minute I step into the steamy, perfumed bath, I relax and quickly feel my body melt like ice on a grill. I have candles lit and I'm listening to Mary J. Blige's CD *The Breakthrough*. I lay my head back, close my eyes, and breathe in her energy, her strength. *Somehow, I have to find a way to break these emotional chains that keep me feeling shackled*, I think. Hot tears begin to singe my eyes, and I let the flames of my pain roll down my face unchecked.

My thoughts start to slowly ripple in my head. My mind begins to swell as a current of questions swish and splash against the melody of the music, against the impossibilities of my marriage. Damn you, Randy! Is it impossible to love me, and accept me, for me? Is it impossible to allow me to love myself? Is it impossible to give you all of my love without being taken for granted, without being taken advantage of? Is it impossible for me to love you without you trying to control how I do it? Is it impossible for me to be inspired, encouraged and emotionally supported by you completely? Is it impossible to be loved without conditions, without being stripped of my self-worth and identity?

When the album finishes, the water is almost cold and I still have no answers. I leave my private sanctuary feeling more uncertain than better, and decide it's time to curl up in front of the television with a hot cup of green tea and the remote. I dry myself off and stand in front of my floor-length mirror, studying my body. Lightly run my fingers along the stretch marks that have become my badge of motherhood. They wrap the front of my lower stomach like thin, spidery fingers. I smile faintly at the image before me: full breasts, flat stomach, and wide hips. Except for my trail of stretch marks, there are women who'd probably kill to have my shape. Still, I find no solace in this. I sigh deeply. I brush my hair, pull it up in a ponytail, and slip on my favorite white silk robe, then blow out the candles and prepare to go downstairs to the kitchen.

I'm a bit surprised when I step into the bedroom and see Randy sprawled out in the middle of our king-size bed with the lights dimmed. He's bare-chested and wearing a mischievous smirk. I glance at the thick patch of curly hair that rests in the center of his chest, then shift my eyes away. I become distracted and have forgotten my destination. I walk into the sitting room adjoining our bedroom.

"I was wondering when you were gonna come up outta there," he says. I try to ignore the sly grin that parts his full lips.

"I thought you'd still be downstairs," I respond, quickly moving across the room. My feet sink into the plushy carpet.

"I decided to turn in early," he replies, "so I can spend some time with my wife." What he says does not hold my interest. I'm looking for my remote. Somehow, it's not where I usually keep it. I walk back into the bedroom, annoyed. Randy is now out of the bed, standing in the nude. The gas fireplace is on. He turns and faces me; his semi-erection curves slightly to the right. I understand clearly. He wants to be fulfilled tonight.

He walks over to me, unties my robe and lets it fall from my shoulders. Randy steps into me and kisses my neck, then my shoulder. I don't stop him. I want to, but I allow him to grab me by the hand and pull me toward the bed. If I protest, it'll turn into an all-night argument with accusations of infidelity. I'm not up for being kept up all night, trying to defend myself. I am not interested in being pinned down and having him take what he believes is his. So I submit.

He hovers over my body. His hands knead my breasts, then he leans down and wraps his warm lips around my erect nipple. My body contradicts what's going on in my head. It responds to his touch, defying my thoughts, ignoring my feelings. I don't want this. Not tonight. I just want to sip a cup of tea and lose myself in front of the TV. I want to say this, but can't. Somehow I have lost my voice. His tongue flicks across my neck, then lightly brushes my earlobe. I spread my legs open, forgetting what I want.

He's inside of me now, moving his hips slowly at first. Then he picks up the pace and deepens his stride, pounding the width and length of himself into a valley slick with apprehension. "Damn, baby, this shit is good. You got my pussy nice and wet;

just how I like it." Randy enjoys talking dirty during sex; says it turns him on. "Yeah, baby," he grunts. His face is slick with sweat. His eyes have become lust-filled slits. "That's it, baby, wet Daddy's dick."

The headboard begins to knock the wall as he's thrusting voraciously. Finally, my voice comes, full of lust, and I'm moaning. I hold on to my husband. Pull him into my essence. Give him all of me, the way he expects. The way I'm supposed to. But, somehow, it doesn't seem to be enough. Still, in the deep space of my heart, I desperately want it to be. With all my might, I match his rhythm, trying to close the chasm between us, squeezing. I love him. I do. But I don't love what my life has become. I'm drowning in pleasure colored with splashes of guilt and self-doubt. His penis is harder than steel and feels heavy inside of me. But I accept his enormous manhood, wrapping my legs around his waist. Despite myself, I pull in my bottom lip and come in a thunderous explosion.

Tonight, he's full of energy.

Deep stroking.

Pumping.

Pounding.

He seems content to spend all night inside of me. I'm getting dizzy, seeing stars. And I wonder how much more I can take before I end up screaming at the top of my lungs. I don't want this. Honestly, I don't. But it's starting to feel good. No, better than good…great. My moans deepen. I grab his tight, muscular behind, pulling him in, gripping him. "This is my pussy," he says, panting, moaning in my ear. "This pussy belongs to me." My body tenses as his thrusts become fast and furious. His body quivers, his eyes roll and sweat drips as he releases his lust-filled loins.

"You mean everything to me, baby," he says breathlessly. He stares deep into my eyes when he says this. There's a hint of desperation in his tone. "I don't know what I'd do if you ever tried to leave me." The notion fills me with angst. I hold my breath and close my eyes, hoping he doesn't see the fear that rapidly flows through me. Surprisingly, he's aroused again, and slipping himself back inside of me. I'm exhausted. But I'm aware it doesn't matter. It never does. So I accept the inevitable and let him take me all over again. It'll be a while before I can get some sleep. And even then, I'll have to keep one eye open.

What does Syreeta want for Syreeta? The question sticks to my brain like glue. And underneath the weight of my husband, in between his grunts and groans, I struggle to peel it apart, to find the answer.

Four

I open my eyes, stretch, and listen to the sounds of Saturday morning. Randy's light snores hum in my ear. The triplets—Karon, Kason, and Kavon—are in my sitting room, laughing and running around, watching their favorite DVD *Shrek*. I inhale their innocence, then wonder where K'wan and Kyle are. *Probably down in the media room, eyes glued to the TV, playing one of their latest video games,* I think with a faint smile. I question what the future holds for my boys who will one day become men. Will my staying in this unhappy situation be the gateway to them becoming lost? Will their personalities and realities about life become hardened by bitterness? Will rage and jealousy consume them? Will distorted ideas of masculinity cloud their judgments? Will they dream, and wonder, and think, and feel, and become unrealistic visions of manhood? I truly hope not. I pray for my sons. I pray that they develop an understanding and knowledge of who they are, of who they should be. I pray that they develop the kind of consciousness that allows them to become loving, respecting men. I pray. And I pray. And I pray.

Slowly I get up, careful not to wake Randy. He nestles deeper into the bed, and spreads his legs wide across the pillow-topped mattress, oblivious to my departure. I steal a glance at him before slipping on my robe. Despite his chiseled features and amazing sex appeal, the richness of his chocolate skin is the only thing perfect under the damask comforter. That much I know. I head for the bathroom, then shut the door. I catch my reflection in the mirror and try to imagine what my life would have been like had I not gotten pregnant and married but pursued a career first. Guilt ripples through me. Yet, I continue to wonder. Like a leech sucking its prey's blood, the masquerade slowly drains the life out of me. It exhausts me. I run my fingers through my shoulder-length hair, then pull it up and turn sideways, catching my profile. I study the smoothness of my soft skin, the natural arch of my brows, the flat mole over my right eye. I am trying to see myself before marriage and children. But everything is a blur. I used to know myself. But in a flash, I have become someone else. Someone unfamiliar—an image of someone else's making. I probe my features a second longer, then start brushing my teeth and washing my face.

When I am done, I gather the triplets using hushed tones, shut off the TV, and head downstairs to make breakfast. The triplets have requested pancakes, eggs, and turkey sausage. I make my way around the kitchen; then, when everything is ready, I call for Kyle and K'wan to come upstairs.

"Wash your hands," I instruct them, pointing toward the bathroom. They go grumbling, then return drying their hands with paper towels. I shake my head, smiling at my little men. I revel in their handsomeness with skin the color of milk chocolate; they have my eyes, and Randy's nose and lips. I can already tell they will have his height as well. We say grace, then eat. The two oldest scarf down their food, anxious to return to the game room. The triplets eat with their fingers and make their usual mess. Today I don't feel like fussing with them to use their forks. I let them be. And allow my thoughts to consume me. They crash together and explode into pellets, causing my head to throb. *What does Syreeta want for Syreeta?* The question unpacks itself and takes up residence in my mind. Crowding me. Letting me know it's here to stay until I find the answer. Sorrowfully, I'm having troubling conceptualizing an existence outside of the one I already have. I shut my eyes and say a quick prayer, trying to will the throbbing away. I have so much to be thankful for. And I am grateful for what I have. But...I have nothing for *me. What does Syreeta want for Syreeta?* This weighs heavily on me. Am I wrong for wanting more? Am I wrong for wanting something for me? If only I could look deep into the eyes of the unknown. Perhaps then I'd see the answers I seek.

"Slow down," I finally say, turning my attention to K'wan and Kyle. "Those games aren't going anywhere."

"But I'm beating K'wan," Kyle states with a mouthful of food.

"Don't talk with your mouth full," I say.

"Only by a hundred points. Big deal," K'wan huffs. "Besides, I'm letting you win."

"Yeah, right," Kyle challenges. "I've beaten you twice already."

"Well, winning isn't everything," I offer. "It's how you play the game."

They both look at me as if I've said something foreign, shaking their heads. "That's because you're a girl," Kyle replies, grinning.

I offer a slight smile and wonder where this belief originated. I decide to challenge his thinking another time.

When everyone is finished eating, I clear the table, clean up the trail of food the triplets have left behind, send them downstairs with Kyle, then begin rinsing the dishes and stacking them in the dishwasher.

The phone rings.

"I'll get it!" yells K'wan, running toward its shrill. He says this before I can dry my hands and make my way to pick up the cordless on the kitchen table.

"Okay," I answer. "And stop running."

"Mommy, phone," he says.

"Who is it?" I ask.

"Aunt Janie."

Janie is my older sister, four years my senior. She lives in Charlotte, North Carolina with her husband, Rodney, and their two children, Simone and Eddie. She, too, married her first love—her college sweetheart. He's a pediatric neurosurgeon at Charlotte General, and she's an interior designer. She's active in her sorority and a proud member of the Links and Jack & Jill. Like me, she lives in a big, beautiful house. The only difference is hers is filled with love while mine contains uncertainty. She's happy with her life. And I'm still searching.

"Okay, honey. Tell her to hold on."

I finish rinsing the last dish, wipe my hands, then walk over to the table and pick up. "Hello?"

"Hey, lady," she chimes.

"Hey," I say back, sitting at the table. "How's the party planning coming?"

"I have the caterer, DJ, the florist, and photographer all lined up. All I need now is my outfit."

"That's fantastic."

"Girl, Mom is going to be really surprised."

"I know. I can't wait to see the expression on her face. I wish I could have done more," I say apologetically.

"That's all right. Just knowing you and the boys will be here is enough. I know you have your hands full, so I understand." She says this in a tone filled with secret connotation. As if she knows more than I've made her privy to. I love my sister, and we're relatively close. But there are some things about my life I choose to keep from her. "So, how's everything going?" she asks, shifting to safer territory. "I mean, with you, Randy, and my handsome nephews?"

"We're all doing well."

"Hmm," she says as if she's half-believing me. But I stick to my truth. For the most part, we *are* doing well. "That's good. I can't wait to see you."

"Me either," I state, smiling. "How are Rodney and the kids?"

"Rodney's doing fine. He's away in the Bahamas on a golf trip. And Simone—as long as she has the phone glued to her ear, is on the Internet, or has her music blaring—is doing great." She shares how my sixteen-year-old niece is growing into a woman before her eyes and becoming a rebel in her quest for independence. I chuckle, remembering Janie when she was that age. Sneaking out through windows. Skipping school. Getting fake IDs to get into the clubs in New York. "Don't even say it," she snaps, joining in my laughter. "I know, I know. This is my punishment. Thank God for Eddie. He's the only one with some sense around here." She chuckles. "Give him a football or basketball and he's content."

"For now," I suggest. "Just wait until he starts to take notice of the opposite sex."

"Hey, don't jinx me," she says jokingly. We share in a sisterly laugh.

Randy walks into the kitchen barefoot and in his pajama bottoms. His blue terrycloth bathrobe hangs open. He shoots me a look I try to ignore. He doesn't like me being on the phone when he's home. He feels my attention should be on him.

"I'll call you back later," I abruptly tell Janie.

"Randy must be up."

"Yeah."

"Humph. Well, make sure you do. Love you."

"I love you, too."

"Good morning," I say, hanging up the phone.

He walks over and plants a kiss on my forehead. "Morning," he says as he heads toward the refrigerator, takes out a carton of orange juice, then pours it into a crystal tumbler.

He sits down opposite me and takes a quick swallow of his juice. "So...who was that?" he asks.

"Janie," I offer.

His attitude immediately changes.

"What'd she want?"

"She wanted to discuss my mother's party, and to find out when I'd get there."

He finishes his drink and gets up from the table, moving toward the sink. "What party?" he asks with his back turned to me. He pulls a glass plate down from the cabinet, then shovels some eggs and four sausages on his plate.

"Her surprise birthday party, remember?"

"No," he says flatly.

"I told you about it three months ago."

"I don't recall you mentioning it."

"Well, I did," I say.

"No," he states, turning around. He leans on the counter and crosses his arms. "You thought you did. But, as always, you like keeping things from me," he says, accusation coursing through his voice.

"That's not true," I say as I massage my forehead. My head throbs along with his sudden shift in disposition.

"Humph," he grunts, turning his back to me again.

"Well, the party is in April...um, Saturday the twenty-ninth," I offer, getting up from the table. For some reason anxiety finds its way into my stomach and settles there, causing me to dart my eyes around the room.

"And?"

I swallow. "And...the boys and I will be leaving that Friday to fly down."

"They can't go," he snaps, rummaging through the refrigerator. The door slams. His back is still toward me, and I am annoyed that he doesn't have the decency to at least look at me.

"What do you mean, 'they can't go'? My family is looking forward to seeing them."

"Just what I said," he replies.

I am baffled. "And why's that?"

Randy finally faces me and speaks slowly and clearly, so there's no misunderstanding. "I'm saying this once, and *only* once. My boys aren't going anywhere near those people." His tone is riddled with disgust. It hovers in the air like smog. My stomach shifts, and I feel my voice catch in the center of my throat. He steps toward me for effect, but I stand my ground, feeling defiant. And cough up the nerve to speak.

"They are my children, too. And *those* people—as you call them—are my family, and theirs," I declare.

"I don't give a damn whose family they are. As long as I pay the bills in this house, you'll do as I say."

I feel like I've been slapped. "Excuse me?"

"I didn't stutter. I *said* they're not going."

I look at him and I suddenly realize I don't know who he is.

This stranger before me is not my husband. Not the man with whom I have spent most of my life. I sigh. "Randy, you don't have to speak to me like I'm some child."

"Well, if you listened, I wouldn't have to talk to you like one."

"Listen, sweetheart," I say, trying to defuse the situation. "I don't want to argue—"

He frowns. "Don't 'sweetheart' me. We wouldn't be arguing if you weren't always trying to do things behind my back."

I shake my head, confused. "I haven't done anything behind your back. I just assumed...I mean, thought, you'd remember and it wouldn't be a problem."

"See. That's your problem. You're always thinking something stupid, and assuming things. And, once again, you've made an ass out of yourself."

"Randy, please don't call me names," I say.

His six-foot frame stiffens. "I'll call you what I want. I *am* the man of this house and what I say goes. So you make sure you let your family know there's been a change in plans."

"But I made the reservations already."

"Then you need to cancel them."

"I can't."

"Syreeta, you heard what I said. Cancel them, and that's that."

"The tickets are nonrefundable, Randy."

"That's just great." He snorts. "More money tossed down the drain. You should have asked before you went and made reservations."

"I didn't think I would need to get your permission to spend time with my family."

"Oh really," he snaps. "If I'm paying for it, you do. As a matter of fact, anything you do needs my permission but I guess you've forgotten that, now that I let you go off to your little counseling sessions."

I want to end this before it escalates. Before he says things he will not be able to retract. Again, I feel responsible for keeping this from turning into a war of words that will be twisted and misinterpreted; words that will become weapons of emotional destruction. "Fine," I say, sighing. "I'll pay the bill."

"Either you're hard of hearing or too stupid to understand, but you're not taking them. And you're not going, either."

I want to back down, accept what he says. But I can't. This is too important to me.

"Randy," I say softly. "It'll only be for a few days."

His face is twisted with rage. "Do you need the wax cleaned out your damn ears, or are you really too dense to comprehend?!!" he shouts. "I *said* they're not going!"

His question punctures me. Stabs me in an unhealed wound. I try to ignore it. I close my eyes, bite my lower lip, and take a long, deep breath.

"My family hasn't seen the kids, or *me*, in almost two years."

"That's not my problem." He scowls. "If they want to see my sons, then they need to come here. 'Cause that's the only way they'll see 'em. And that's that."

"I don't see what the big deal is."

"Look, woman. I'm not going to keep going back and forth with you."

Despite his tone, in spite of the way his jaws tighten, I still feel the need to push the envelope one last time. "We're only going for the weekend."

"You already heard what I said. Don't make me have to repeat myself."

I don't want to go against my husband, but I cannot let this go. I want to see my family. And my family wants to see me. Not going is not an option, not one I am willing to accept. I cannot create excuses to explain my absence, at least none that will be believable. "Randy, please. We'll be back Sunday afternoon. I promise."

"Syreeta, I'm warning you."

My heart is beating fast and I have no idea what I will do if this escalates, as it has done in the past when I don't acquiesce. Defiance gets the best of me. I thrust out my chin. "Or what?"

He steps closer. "Or…you can pack your shit, and get out!" His spittle sprays my face.

I am not prepared for what he has said. His words sting and I'm stunned. Randy knows I have no money and no viable place to go. I look at him with hurt eyes. Tears gather in the corners of them but don't fall. Our eyes lock—mine full of pain, his, disdain.

He slams his plate to the floor. The glass shatters as eggs and sausage hit the white marble. "Make yourself useful!" he bellows. "And clean this mess up!"

I am frozen in place, scared of what he will do next and hoping the boys haven't heard him. However, as loud as he is, I know that's just wishful thinking.

His piercing eyes stick me like thorns. Inside, I'm trembling as he stares hard at me. I want to challenge him, tell him the boys are going no matter what he says. Tell him to clean up his own damn mess. But I don't. He looks me up and down with contempt painted on his face before storming out, leaving me shaking with anger.

Five

Randy is locked away in his study and the boys are down-stairs as I prepare dinner.

I'm busying myself around the kitchen. I wash lettuce, cut up red onions, dice tomatoes and slice cucumbers for the salad. I've made smothered chicken with brown rice and broccoli. I take out plates and get glasses to set the table, and lay out napkins. When everything is ready, I call for my sons to come eat. Then I knock on the double mahogany doors that separate Randy from the rest of the house. "Dinner's ready," I say, opening the door. Something rustles inside of me. My feelings are still bruised from earlier. I am angry and sad. And I can't help but wonder how much more of his emotional annihilations I can endure.

"I'll be out in a minute," he responds. His back remains turned toward the door as his thick fingers click the keys of his laptop. I silently close the door and return to the kitchen.

No one lifts a fork until Randy comes to the table. It's a rule he imposes, and enforces. When he finally sits at the table, everyone eats in silence except the triplets, who are whining and picking at their food. Without naps, they are cranky. I get up and attempt to console them, try to get them to eat. But it's an uphill battle, one I know I will lose. So, I give in. Like me, they are too tired to be bothered. I wipe their mouths and faces, release them from their chairs, and allow them to wander off. I am surprised Randy doesn't say something to me for allowing them to not finish their food. Any other time, he'd tell me to let them be; to let them sit in their chairs until we were all done eating; to stop babying them. But tonight, he says nothing.

Across the table, I feel him snatching looks at me. His eyes are filled with a yearning I don't share. Eyes that eagerly await attention and acknowledgment, shimmering with lust; not the same eyes I once looked into and saw beautiful rainbows. My heart aches. I stare past him, still stuck on this morning's events. Words said, threats made, that he has surely forgotten. But they remain stubbornly rooted in my memory.

As I load the dishwasher and wash pots, scrub the stove, wipe counters, sweep and mop the floor; as I bathe the triplets and tuck them in, and direct our two oldest sons to get ready for bed, I feel his smoldering, endless gaze on me.

❖❖❖

I am awakened when I hear Randy's voice, and feel his hands roaming my body, finally resting on my breast. "Syreeta?" He squeezes my nipple, then slides his hand over the curve of my hip and hikes up my nightgown. His manhood, thick and eager, presses against me, rock hard. *Not tonight*, I mutter in my head. *I'm tired.* I try to force the words out, but they are stuck somewhere in the back of my throat. I remain still. Shut my eyes tighter. Hope he gets the subtle hint. "I know you're not sleep," he says, gently shaking me. He pulls down the strap of my nightgown and kisses my shoulder and back. I let out a frustrated sigh which he mistakes for pleasure. "You know you want me inside of you, and you know I'll take it if I have to. You want me to take it, don't you?"

I ignore him. Continue pretending. Yes, I know my husband will have his way with me whether I want him to or not. He will force himself on me as he has many times before without ever thinking of it as rape. I roll over, adjust my eyes to the darkness and stare at him, through him. It's always about what he wants. As always, I accept this to be true, and spread open my legs, too exhausted to resist. He roughly pulls my panties aside, places his face between my legs, then licks the center of my sex. His tongue reaches for something buried, determined to find what's missing. Something I've tried to keep hidden. He explores my essence. Teases my spot. Slowly, I surrender to the stirring between my legs. When I am slick, he jams himself deeply inside me. A moan gushes out of me. And before I know what's come over me, I am matching his thrusts. Squeezing him. Getting lost in his rhythm. Desperately needing, and wanting, a perfect love.

He pulls out of me. "Turn over and get on your knees." His voice is raspy and commanding. I do as I am told. He slips himself back inside of me. His length fills me to capacity; his thickness stretches me. He begins pumping me wildly, intermittently slapping my behind. His slaps sting my flesh. I'm on the brink of tears. Pleasure begins to border on pain. He's hurting me. There is no passion behind his thrust, just sex. But I allow him to have his way. "You want Daddy to bury this nut in you," he pants, slapping my behind again. "Don't you?" I stifle a scream. "This how you want it, baby?" He thrusts deep in me, hitting my spot, stoking a fire inside of me. "You love this dick. You want all this fat dick?" My mind is racing a mile a minute. He is yanking me by the hair; his sweat drips onto my back, as he loses himself in me. "I want you pregnant tonight," he says in a deep, husky voice. "This ass belongs to me." He pounds himself in and out. Fast and furious, he is riding me mercilessly. Tonight, Randy is on a mission. One he intends to complete. A single tear escapes my eye and slides down my face. I close my eyes, bury my face into the mattress, and grab the edge of the bed, expanding and contracting until he spills himself deep inside of me, planting seeds of hopelessness.

❖❖❖

The room is visited by an unfamiliar silence. The past and present intertwine, then loop themselves around the future. Instinctively, I look up and see a knot of uncertainty hovering over my head like a noose. Effortlessly, I hold my breath and wait for it to gradually find its way around my neck. And it does.

"I've decided you can go visit your family with the boys," Randy tells me as he's lying on his back, arms bent behind his head, looking up at the ceiling. I turn to look at him, not sure of what to say. My mind has already been made up. I am going anyway, no matter what he has said. But I don't tell him this.

"Thank you," I say, not feeling the least bit thankful. Somehow I know this privilege will come with a price. Somehow I know that this bone, as quick as it has been thrown, will be snatched away without warning.

"You can go under one condition," he says, pausing. He is baiting me, waiting for me to bite. And I do.

"What's that?" I ask nervously.

"That we have a threesome," he states. His request sounds like a demand. And knowing my husband, it is. I take a moment to catch my breath, then sit up.

For a split second, I think I'm lost. I'm in the wrong house, sitting up in the wrong bed, looking at the wrong man. There's no way I hear him correctly. But my ears aren't playing tricks on me. I know what I heard. He wants a ménage à trois. I blink, blink again, trying to register his statement.

"Excuse me?" I ask incredulously.

"I want a threesome," he says evenly.

"Wait a minute. So, you're telling me that the only way I can go to my mother's surprise party is by agreeing to participate in sex with you and another woman?"

He looks at me as if what he has requested makes sense. "Yeah," he says. "What's wrong with that?"

"What's wrong with it?" I repeat, trying to keep my tone steady. "I am your wife. I can't believe you'd suggest sleeping with another woman. Where's this coming from?" I ask.

"It's something I've always fantasized about," he explains. "I want to try something different. And I think it's time we explore it." I am crushed. I should be enough. But he says if I love him, then I'd be open to it. If I cared anything about our marriage, I'd do whatever it took to keep him happy. My face feels flushed. *Haven't I already done enough?* I think. I consider myself open to most things. This is where I draw the line.

"No," I say.

His face tightens. "What?"

"I said *no*. I won't do it." My tone is final. But I know Randy. He will not let it go. He will continue pulling, tearing my decision apart, until he gets what he wants. But, this is one fight he will not win. Not tonight, or any other night.

"I thought you wanted to go visit your family."

"I will...I mean, I do," I state, catching myself. "But not at the expense of allowing you to have another woman in our bed."

"And why not?" he asks.

"Because I don't feel that it's right."

"You need to loosen up," he snaps. "What are you so afraid of?"

I shake my head. "Nothing," I state. "I just don't think bringing someone else into our bed is a good idea."

He snorts. "You need to stop being such a prude."

"I'm not being a prude. I'm just not comfortable with the idea of you being with another woman."

"This is not about me being with another woman. It's about us exploring alternatives together; about us being more adventurous."

I almost want to laugh at his reasoning. Its absurdity. But I am too shocked. Adventure is going on a camping trip, sky diving, or climbing the Alps. Not asking your wife, the mother of your children, to engage in a threesome with another woman. I wonder if he'd be so willing to explore this kind of adventure if I said I wanted to bring another man into our bed. Would he be the least bit fazed by such a ridiculous request? I stop myself from asking, knowing it's something I'd never want or consider anyway.

I sigh, shaking my head. "I won't."

The temperature in the room drops ten degrees as he turns his stare toward me. "Maybe if you weren't so frigid, I wouldn't have these thoughts," he snaps. The coldness in his voice sends chills up my spine.

I am insulted. "I'm not frigid," I say, folding my arms defiantly across my chest.

He sits up in bed. "Like hell you aren't. When's the last time you initiated sex? Don't you think I'd like to lie back and be pleased sometimes?"

His question offends me. "I *have* initiated it, Randy. And every time I do you say no. It always has to be on your terms. How do you think that makes me feel?"

He rolls his eyes up in his head. "Oh, please. I told you no once because I had to get up early for a meeting. Why do you always have to exaggerate things?"

Once again, Randy will try to make me feel as if I am making a mountain out of a molehill, embellishing the truth according to him. I stay focused. Don't allow him to lure me into his mental trap. "No, Randy, it's not an exaggeration. It's a reality. On more than one occasion I've wanted to make love to you or just be held. And you pushed me off of you, or turned on your side because you didn't feel like being bothered."

"Well, maybe you should try to do something to get me in the mood more often."

"I've tried," I say in a voice that sounds pleading, more desperate than I intend.

He rolls his eyes. "Oh, please," he snaps.

"Randy, in all the years we've been married, I have never denied you. Anytime you want sex, I give it to you. No questions asked. Not once have I turned you down. Even when I'm not in the mood or don't feel like it."

His jaws tighten. "And what in the hell do you mean by that? Don't act like you're doing me some big favor."

"That's not what I'm saying."

"Well, that's what it sounds like to me."

Somehow, I know this conversation will be turned around. He will make me feel like I'm the problem. I tread, knowingly. "Randy, I don't want to argue with you. I'm just making a point."

"And your point is?"

"That I'm your wife. And I do what is necessary to satisfy you. Sometimes you have to do things you don't always feel like doing to keep your partner happy. "

He laughs. "Oh, is that so?"

"Yes."

He sucks his teeth. "Okay then, tell me. When's the last time you got on your knees and sucked my dick?"

I cringe. His question catches me off guard. He's talking to me like I'm some common whore. "Excuse me?" I manage, breathing in the remnants of hot, sweaty air.

"When's the last time you sucked my dick without me having to ask you to?" he repeats, glaring at me.

My eyes narrow, my lips purse. I try to understand where his question is heading. Try to figure out what's brought on this attitude. But I know there's no telling. Like the wind, this conversation will blow in a direction beyond my control. I ponder what he has asked. Performing oral sex on him doesn't repulse me. It's how he wants me to do it. How he takes me by the back of my head and tries to choke me with his penis. It's like he enjoys trying to ram himself down my throat, enjoys seeing me gagging and choking. I feel he gets off seeing tears surface in my eyes as he blocks my airway. I know he knows it's not something I enjoy. But I do it because I love him. Because it's what *he* enjoys. Because it keeps him from turning the night into an argument filled with accusations and insults.

His question takes me back to the four months I spent confined to bed rest during my pregnancy with the triplets because of bleeding. When the doctor finally recommended that we abstain from sexual relations until after their birth, Randy decided I should still please him orally. The first night he insisted on oral sex, he stood in front of me, rubbed his penis across my mouth, and when I opened my mouth to receive him, he dipped at the knees and moved himself in and out of my mouth, then grabbed the back of my head and began pushing the length of himself to the back of my throat slowly at first, then forcefully. He ignored my gagging, overlooked my tears, pushed my hands away when I tried to hold him at the base to gain some control, then became enraged when I threw up all over him.

"Randy, you know how I feel about that," I say. "I don't mind performing oral sex as long as you aren't so rough."

"Yeah, right," he huffs. "Most of the time you act like you're scared of it. And when you do finally put your mouth around it, you refuse to swallow my nut when I cum. I eat you, don't I?"

I turn away, pressing back an avalanche of hurt.

"Answer me," he snaps.

I nod.

"And don't I make you feel good?"

I feel like a child being scolded for misbehaving. "Yes," I manage in a tone barely audible. I say this in a voice that doesn't belong to me.

"Well, why can't I get the same thing? You're my wife. You should be sucking my dick like you love it. Instead, I get lousy-ass head. You're lazy in bed. And you talk about you do what's necessary to satisfy me. Give me a break. If you really want to satisfy me, then all I'm asking is for some head from my wife from time to time without me having to ask for it; give me the pussy like you mean it. And for us to have a simple threesome. I don't think that's a lot to ask. I have never cheated on you. But if you don't start getting with the program, you'll have no one to blame but yourself."

Taken aback, I begin to say something, but no words leave my mouth. I feel the bile rising. I am sick to my stomach. I watch as Randy gets out of bed, slips into pajama bottoms, and storms out of the room. He slams the door, leaving behind a trail of guilt that shouldn't be left for me. Anger is floating around me. I attempt to shoo it away, but it keeps buzzing around like a pesky fly. I stare at the door, unsettled. I count to one hundred, forward and backward. Wait for the door to reopen and Randy to reappear, shouting, "April fools!" even though I know it's not April. Wait for him to come back and say, "Baby, I was just talking out my head. You know how much I love you. You're the only woman I need. You keep me more than satisfied."

He doesn't.

I toss and turn most of the night. I'm running on quicksand. Being pulled into something that feels beyond my control. Hands of uncertainty are grabbing at my feet. I'm gasping, trying to catch my breath. My lungs tighten. The thumping in my heart is unbearable. I awaken drenched in sweat, try to adjust my eyes to the darkness. Randy's side of the bed is still empty. It's obvious he's made himself comfortable in one of the guest rooms. I wipe tears from my face and glance at the digital clock on his side of the room. 2:40 a.m. I get out of bed and make my way to the bathroom.

I turn on the shower, and when the steam covers the glass doors, I step in and allow the pulse to caress my wounded soul. When I am finished, I dry myself off, find a clean nightgown, change the sheets, then climb back in bed. I don't sleep, don't move, just lie there listening to the whir of the ceiling fan. Loneliness slowly smothers me. I can't breathe. I don't want to be me anymore. Don't want this life. Don't want to keep pretending. I don't want to cry. But…the wells of my eyes overflow, the walls of my heart crack, and the tears crash against my pillow, dragging me with its undertow. Tossing my life around, flooding the space between Randy and me.

Six

I can't stand this silence, this stillness. It hovers in the air and stifles me. My lungs burn breathing in the thick emptiness that has become the air I am forced to breathe. I hate this state of isolation. As far as I'm concerned, being hit is far better than the feeling of being disregarded and rejected by someone you love.

It's been two days since Randy stormed out of our bedroom because I refused to give in to his sick, twisted request to participate in a ménage á trois. He is still not speaking to me, and I am still not willing to change my mind. Despite his threat to cheat, despite him withdrawing his attention, I am rooted in my decision. As a result, I have become invisible to him. I have been relegated to oblivion; forced to be unseen and unheard. Randy has drawn a line, and has forbidden me to cross it. And I won't. Not until he invites me back into his space.

Funny thing, I should be used to this, should be immune to his detachment, but I am not. It still hurts. I don't think I can ever get used to being treated as if I don't exist, as if I am not worthy of existing. And the thing that's most disturbing, most frightening for me, is that there's a part of me that wishes he would just yell and scream and curse me out. As crazy as it sounds, I would rather be bruised and bleeding than be subjected to what I am feeling now, which is insignificant. Just call me a slew of degrading names, slap me around, then be done with it. Instead, he has made the choice to ignore me. I will continue to go unnoticed until Randy decides that I have been punished enough.

Reflection claims me, and I start to ponder why Randy married me. Out of all the women whom he could have had, why was I the chosen one? Was it because I wore my heart on my sleeve for him? Because my love for him was endless? Or was it that I was easy prey; could he sense my vulnerabilities? Had he recognized that he would be able to easily mold, shape, and bend me into whatever he believed I should be? Had he orchestrated this journey from the beginning, knowing that he would be able to control me? That my existence would become completely dependent upon his? Did he already know that he would pull me down and drag me emotionally and mentally into a hole so deep that I would never see my way out? The reasonable part of my mind tells me that if I am to ever find the misplaced pieces of my life, I have to find a way to get out of this, to free myself from the man I love. Yet my heart, the muscle that pumps and beats and controls my sensibilities says: *You can't.* And it is in the strength of those words, the glue that keeps me cemented, that I accept this as truth, and stay.

❖❖❖

I am in the midst of cooking dinner when I hear the alarm chirp, alerting me that someone has entered the house. I know it is Randy without seeing or hearing him. I glance up at the wall clock. It reads 5:45 p.m. I hear his muffled footsteps and know he is heading upstairs. He will take his shower, then retreat to his office. He will take no notice of me, and most likely say very little to his sons. I finish glazing the salmon, then place it back in the oven. He wants, no, expects dinner to be ready by the time he finishes his fifteen-minute shower. I turn the flame down on the stove, then scramble to finish the garden salad and set the table. Cooking is not a task I am up for tonight, but I do not want to give Randy any more reason to extend his silent treatment. My life, everything I do, revolves around his moods. And, sadly, I will tiptoe around him until he says otherwise.

When everything is prepared, I call for the boys. Ask K'wan to go upstairs to let his father know dinner is ready. Kavon and Karon are both trying my patience. They are fussy, and I am not in the mood for their whining and falling out. Not today. They have decided they want cereal instead of the spaghetti and meatballs I have made for them. I make two separate meals because Randy doesn't like pasta dishes. He doesn't like anything in a can, won't eat frozen vegetables, hates leftovers. He wants everything fresh, and homemade. "No cereal," I say. "I made you spaghetti. You can have cereal in the morning." They look at me. Try to register what I have offered. When they cannot, they start crying. I ignore them. Turn my back on them. Refuse to feed into it. Somehow I feel like I am treating them the way Randy has been treating me, as though they are—invisible. Guilt causes me to go to them, comfort them. And do what I usually do...struggle not to give in.

K'wan enters the kitchen, his face blank. "Daddy said he's not eating." He watches for my reaction. He knows I have been running around the kitchen trying to make sure dinner is on time. He knows his father's imposed house rule. He knows I have been walking on eggshells. He knows too much. And I refuse to give him more. My eyes sweep the kitchen. Kyle is stealing sly glances at me. He knows, too. The triplets are the only ones unaware of what is going on. I steel myself. Desperately try to maintain my composure under a lid that is about to explode. *Damn him!* I turn from the prying eyes that are watching me and busy myself around the kitchen, wiping down granite countertops that have already been wiped twice. *A whole meal wasted*, I think. I am angry. I want to scream. But I don't. I toss the rag into the sink, pull in a deep breath, then slowly let it out. I turn and face K'wan. "Go wash your hands," I say to him. "It's time to eat."

Seven

The week drifts past me and extends itself into Thursday before I know it. I almost forget about my appointment, but the bold red circle around the date on my calendar reminds me. I hop in my car and speed to my destination. When I arrive, I race up the stairs, glancing at my watch. I am almost fifteen minutes late.

I walk into Dr. Curtis's plush office, wiping a film of sweat from my forehead. He is standing in the waiting area talking to his secretary, a busty caramel-colored woman with beautiful locks down her back, about a cancellation. He looks up and smiles. Its warmth can melt an iceberg. Today, he's wearing a starched white shirt and a pair of hand-tailored, blue, pinstriped pants with a burgundy pinstriped silk tie.

"I'm sorry, Doctor Curtis, I didn't realize how late it had gotten."

"No problem. I wasn't concerned. I knew you'd be here," he says, walking over and extending his large, manicured hand. "My appointment after you just called and canceled, so we have more than enough time. Come on in."

I follow him into his office. His intoxicating scent lingers around my nose. He smells good. "What is that cologne you have on?" I ask, inhaling deeply.

"It's Very Irresistible by Givenchy."

I smile and wonder if my handsome doctor is married. Marvel at what type of woman I imagine he's attracted to. Wonder if he's as gentle in his relationship as he is in his sessions. Not that I'm interested in him, just curious. With the exception of his degrees and numerous awards hanging on the wall, there are no pictures, no telltale signs of family or a life outside of his work. His world is private. His boundaries are clear: no undue familiarity. And I respect that. "It smells nice," I say.

"Thank you. Make yourself comfortable," Dr. Curtis replies, sitting down. I take my seat on the sofa opposite him and cross my legs, clasping my hands firmly in my lap.

"Did you give some thought to what we talked about last week?" he begins, flipping through his notes.

What does Syreeta want for Syreeta? I want to tell him that the question has been nagging at me. Tell him that I feel so lost that I don't know if I'll ever be able to find the answer. "I've been thinking about it," I offer.

"And?"

I shrug, shaking my head.

He nods knowingly. "Don't worry," he says. "The answers will come. So how have you been since our last session?"

"I've had better days."

"Why don't you tell me about it?"

I spend the next twenty minutes telling Dr. Curtis about Randy not wanting me to take our children to visit my family. I tell him about my husband's unnerving split personality, and how he has shut me out. How he wants a threesome. I don't want to reveal too much about what he has asked of me sexually, but I do anyway.

"And how does all this make you feel?" he asks when I finish.

"Angry," I say, "and confused."

"Confused? How so?"

"Randy hasn't spoken to me in almost three days. If he really loves me, why would he want to bring someone else into our bed? Why would he stop talking to me? It's like he's trying to say that I'm not enough woman for him. That how I feel doesn't matter. Yet, almost every night, with the exception of the last few nights, he's either crawling on top of me, or waking me up by fondling all over me. And never have I denied him. No matter how tired I am, no matter how upset I am, no matter how disinterested I am, I am always available to my husband."

"This has nothing to do with love," Dr. Curtis points out. "It's about manipulation. It's about power and control. He knows very well that the last thing you want is for him to have an affair. By making threats and ignoring you, he is trying to plant the seed that any problems in your marriage or with your sex life are your doing. He is skillfully trying to influence you into doing something you don't want to do. The question is, do you think you're not enough woman for your husband?"

"I honestly don't know what to think anymore. I allow him to have me any way he wants because it's what he wants, and because he's my husband."

"Why?"

"Because I love him," I say, wiping tears from my eyes.

"And?"

I hear Randy's voice in my head. *You are my wife. I provide for you, give you everything you need. The very least you can do is keep me satisfied in bed. I don't look at other women, but if you want me to start I will.* "Because it's my duty to please him."

"Your duty? Says who?"

I shift in my seat. "My mother...Randy."

"Syreeta, your duties as a wife have nothing to do with being forced, or coerced, into performing sexual acts that make you uncomfortable. That is just another form of abuse. At any time you should have the right to say no. And you should be able to say it, and mean it, without fear."

"At what cost?" I ask. "If I say no, then I run the risk of my husband going out and finding someone else willing to please him, and do all the things he likes in bed."

"And if you don't, then you continue to feel uncomfortable, and he continues to humiliate and degrade you. What he's doing is called emotional blackmail."

Emotional blackmail, I think. It's a term I have never heard before. But somehow I have become entangled in it. I am anxious to hear more about it. I tilt my head. Wait for his explanation.

He senses this.

"Emotional blackmail is when someone uses manipulation repeatedly to coerce you to comply with their demands at the expense of your own well-being. People who use this tactic will do or say whatever is necessary to instill and/or intensify fear and guilt in you until you eventually give in and comply. When you are resistant to someone's demands, instead of respecting your feelings, they continue to push you to change your mind and if charming you doesn't get them their way, then they escalate to threats that let you know there will be consequences if they don't get what they want. In a healthy relationship, you have a right to set limits and to have your feelings respected."

Maybe if you weren't so frigid. I shake my head. What Dr. Curtis says rings true for me but I am not prepared to embrace it. The thought of Randy being with someone else sexually is too much for me to bear. Infidelity has never been an issue, or a concern. I don't want it to become one now because I pushed the envelope. "I'll just have to relax, and try to be more open," I say.

"And in the end, he continues to win which only reinforces his belief that intimidation and threats get him exactly what he wants."

"Maybe, Doc," I say solemnly, "but at least I don't lose him to another woman."

"But you continue to lose *you* to him in the process."

"Right now," I explain, "I have no other choice."

"At the moment, it's the only option you're able to see. But, in time, another set of choices will come into view."

"I don't know if that'll ever be possible."

"And why's that?" he asks.

I sigh. "I feel like I'm stuck in a thick fog. Everything around me is blurred. The only things I see are splotchy images of my life."

"Tell me about these images," Dr Curtis says, leaning back in his seat.

"I see a clock," I explain. "And I'm the hands on it, helplessly spinning around. When it finally slows down, I jump down, look around, and see time has slipped past me. Then I start running to catch up. But the hands of the clock begin to spin out of control. And the harder I run, the faster time flies by. Finally when the clock stops, I collapse."

"What do you think that means?"

"I wish I knew," I say, exhaling deeply.

"Take a wild guess."

Hopeless…helpless, I think. I'm wrestling with my emotions. Trying to maintain a picture-perfect world has taken a toll on me. I can no longer ignore the truth. I'm being defeated by feelings of guilt, and hurt, and sadness. Like the hands of that clock, my life is spinning out of control. A stream of tears runs silently down my cheeks. I can't bring myself to stop them. Embarrassed, I turn my head, try to hide them, to no avail.

Dr. Curtis reaches over and offers me some tissues. I take them and wipe my face, then blow my nose. "Everything you're feeling is natural. The guilt. The shame. Even embarrassment. But you can't blame yourself for your husband's behavior," Dr. Curtis says. "He's responsible for his actions. You're responsible for your own behavior and the choices you make. It's not your fault that he mistreats you or tries to control and manipulate you. You are worthy of being loved, and being respected. And if he's incapable of doing that, then you—and only you—have to decide how you wish to handle that.

"Whether you stay or decide to leave, the choice is yours alone to make. But whatever you choose, you can learn not to accept anything less than respect. You can demand it. You can claim it. You do not deserve to be abused, used, or mistreated by anyone. You are worthy of receiving love, and giving it in return. Syreeta, no matter how different you want things to be, you can't change anyone. You can only change what you do about it. Regardless of anything else in life, the one thing you always have is choices. We all do. Good, bad, or indifferent. We have the ability to make some decisions for ourselves.

"Sometimes those decisions, the choices we are forced to make, aren't always easy ones. But they're ours. And we need to be able to live with them." Dr. Curtis leans in, looks me directly in the eyes, and says, "No matter what you decide, you can renew your spirit, reclaim your heart, redirect your journey, re-create your image, and embrace a new beginning. No one can rescue you from your current situation, except you. You, Syreeta, have the power to heal. Whether you believe it or not, you can have a voice and take control of your life."

I take more tissue and wipe my eyes. Pull in a deep breath. Dr. Curtis's words console me. His voice is filled with compassion. I hear the ticking, although faint, in my head, but say nothing. I'm grateful, Dr. Curtis allows silence into the room and gives me time to collect myself.

My tears dry. But the sheer monotony of my life has gotten the best of me. "I'm suffocating," I finally admit. "And that frightens me." I shake my head, trying to keep myself from breaking down again. "I love my husband, and I want nothing more than to be happy with him. But just when I think I am, he says or does something that makes me question what we have."

He nods, scribbles something in his notes, then rests his pen to the side, clasping his hands. "No one's happiness should be contingent on another human being. Happiness should come from within."

"I know. But everything I am has been surrounded by him and what we have."

"And what is it you think the two of you have?"

What do I think Randy and I have? The question catches me off guard and I don't know how to reply without sounding very clichéd, because forever is the only thing I ever imagined with Randy; it's the only thing I cling to. What I believe in my heart we'd always have. But now, I can't be so certain.

"We have almost twelve years of marriage and five beautiful children," I respond. I stare at a handsome leather binder on the coffee table, feeling what I've just said isn't enough. "And..."

He picks up his pen, scribbles some more. "Let me rephrase the question," Dr. Curtis says, sensing my loss for words. "What kind of relationship would you say you and your husband have?"

He allows silence to enter the room again. It gives me time to mull over his question.

"Strained," I finally admit.

"And why do you feel it's strained?"

"Because Randy and I don't talk. There's no communication between us. When we do talk it's usually him talking at me, giving me orders or advising me about something. Other than that, I don't know what he's thinking, or feeling. We're like two strangers passing in the night."

"And how does that make you feel?"

"Like I'm not really a part of his world," I say, feeling tears fill my eyes again. "Like our marriage is falling apart."

"Have you told him this?"

There's no way I can bring myself to tell him this. I shake my head. "No."

"Why not?"

"Because I don't want to create any more problems between us," I say softly. "He always thinks I'm looking for things to complain about."

"Is that the real reason?" Dr. Curtis asks.

"Of course," I say quickly. "What other reason would there be?" I ask this, but I know the answer. It's what keeps me in this situation. It paralyzes me. I feel like I'm slowly on the verge of a nervous breakdown. I know Dr. Curtis knows, too. I search his face for expression. There is none. He places his pad in his lap and folds his hands.

"Fear," he says for me. "Am I correct?"

I don't answer. I glance around the room, looking for the

key that will free me from this prison. Sadly, I don't see one. I turn my attention back to Dr. Curtis, hoping he can show me the way to freedom. Dr. Curtis doesn't repeat his question. He doesn't have to. We both already know the answer. I fear the unknown, and the unexpected. I'm not in a position to leave. And if I were, I'm not so sure I'd want to walk away from the life I have. Randy has provided me with a very comfortable lifestyle. If I left him, I'd be leaving with nothing. I am not prepared for any other way of being. He has all the money. How would I care for my children? Where would I go with five kids? These are questions to which I dare not consider the answers. Welfare or being homeless is not a life I'd want for myself, or my children. No. Leaving is *not* the answer, or an option. Despite what my heart feels, we've built a life together. Although it isn't perfect, it's a life I've helped nurture. This life, the one I've helped create, is all I know. It's a world I'm not prepared to run from, not willing to abandon. Despite my confusion, I accept that my life is with my husband no matter what. He's a good man. He would do anything for his family. I'll just have to work harder at keeping him happy. Things between us will get better. Soon. This is what I have to believe.

"Dr. Curtis," I ask, clinging to optimism. "He can change, can't he?"

He leans back in his seat and considers my question. He nods, giving me a slight smile. "To answer your question honestly, abusers *can* change, only if they want to. Only when they choose to; so, yes, your husband can change. But it will mean giving up patterns of behavior, attitudes and beliefs he's held on to, that he's probably had, for a very long time. That kind of change won't come easily. And it definitely won't happen overnight."

The word *abuser* does something to me. Pierces through me

like a hot knife. Its blade, smoldering and jagged, cuts into my heart. Burns deep sores into my soul. I am struggling with this knowledge. Still...I hope.

"But there's still a chance," I say mostly to myself. It is more of a statement than a question. Yet, I wait for Dr. Curtis's answer. Hold on to his every word.

"When he can accept full responsibility for his behavior and stop justifying, rationalizing, and minimizing his abuse, yes, there's hope. But he should be in a batterers' intervention program. Without it," he offers, "the chances of him making any lasting change is slim. Not that intervention guarantees the violence will stop, but it does provide a process for his behavior and beliefs to be challenged, and for him to be held account-able. And it sends a message that abuse of any kind is not acceptable. I just want to reiterate, even if your husband does say he wants to stop his abusive ways and get help, it is still very important for *you* to continue to plan for your safety and that of your children. Like I said before, there really are no guarantees the battering will stop."

Silence enters the space between us.

I steal a peek at my watch. It is almost two p.m. He has allowed me to go over by twenty minutes. Although he hasn't said my time is up, I have to get going. I have to pick up the kids from school and day care, and prepare dinner before Randy gets home. He must sense this. He gets up and eases over to his mahogany desk.

"I have something I want you to read," he says, walking back with two books in his hand. He hands them to me. I look them over. One is titled *Shattered Souls*. The other is titled *Breaking the Cycle* and is a collection of short stories on domestic violence.

"They're fiction, but I think you'll find them both very power-ful readings."

"Thank you. I'll try to start them this weekend."

"Good," he responds, flipping through his calendar. "When you're done reading them, I'd like to talk about what you've read. I'm going to schedule you for next Thursday. The same time."

"Okay," I say, reluctantly moving toward the door, clutching the books to my chest. He smiles and his dimples deepen. I smile back faintly. An unexpected sadness finds me and makes me uneasy. I want to remain hidden. But I can't. I am so torn. But the one thing I'm certain of, what I know in my heart, is that once I walk out of his office, loneliness and despair are on the other side of the door, waiting.

❖❖❖

In the still of the night, the silence between Randy and me is broken. I am not surprised when he awakens me, running his hands along my body, fondling me. His need to fulfill his carnal desires brings him to me, eager and ready. This is how it usually ends. His hardness pressed against me, him wanting to release himself. Thrusting and panting. Moaning and groan-ing. I become the dumping ground for his sexual pleasures. When he is done, he will roll over and drift off to sleep. And in the morning all will be forgotten. He acts as if nothing has been wrong, as if it is normal for two human beings to live under the same roof, sleep in the same bed, and not say one word to each other. This is what he expects me to accept. And I do. As I open my legs and allow him inside of me, I consent to this. I will match his thrusts, orgasm, then force myself to forget how he has made me feel the last few days, and pretend that everything is okay.

❖❖❖

Morning comes in rushed, clipped sounds. The running shower stops, the bathroom door swings open, steam rushes out, dresser drawers open and shut, and Randy is moving about the bedroom. I do not need an alarm clock to know it is almost five a.m. He will be out the door at five-thirty, on his way into the city. And at six, I will get up to make sure K'wan and Kyle are ready for school. I am too exhausted to think about leaving the warm comfort of my bed, let alone opening my eyes to face another day of errands and house chores. All of the other wives in my neighborhood have housekeepers and nannies, and some even have personal drivers, to help them with whatever needs to get done. Like me, none of these women work. And none of them—not that I am aware of—are isolated, except for me. A part of me is envious that they have the freedom to go to salon spas, to luncheons, and on shopping sprees while I am expected to tend to the demands of a husband and five children. *That's what a wife is supposed to do. Not sitting around gossiping all day and spending her husband's money, well, not in my house anyway.*

Randy plants a kiss on the side of my face. I stir under the covers, open my eyes, see him hovering over me. "It's almost time to get up," he says. I inhale. Breathe in his presence. He smells like a tropical paradise; a mixture of Dial soap and Pleasures for Men greets me. "I need you to drop off the pile of shirts in the middle of my closet floor at the dry cleaners today, all right?" I blink, blink again. It isn't a question, so I don't bother telling him what I'm really thinking. *No, take them yourself!*

I nod. "All right," I say, shifting in bed. I am so drained, mentally and emotionally weary. I do not want to play superwoman today. Do not want to be bombarded with demands. Not today. I am tired, tired, tired! And, for some reason, I feel like screaming at the top of my lungs, feel like standing up in the center of my bed and jumping up and down in defiance; yelling to the high heavens for someone to come take me away.

"I'll call you later," he says as he heads out of the bedroom. I glance over at the clock on the nightstand. It reads 5:27 a.m.

There are only thirty—maybe forty-five if I push it—minutes left before my daily routine begins. I pull in a deep breath. Yank the covers up over my head. Wonder if I am the only one in this community of neatly coiffed, designer-clad women trapped in fantasy.

I think that at some point in every woman's life she has had dreams of finding her very own Prince Charming; her knight in shining armor. Someplace, buried deep in her spirit, she yearns for a man with whom she can share her life, giving him her mind, body and soul; the man who will capture her heart and give her an idyllic, picture-perfect, fairy-tale life. I believe this. She believes this. And like I have, she holds on to this. But, then she awakens, opens her eyes, and realizes that perfect doesn't exist. That fairy tales are only in story books. That dreams don't always come true. That love isn't always magical. And that her knight's armor isn't all that shiny. Painfully, regretfully, unwillingly, she sees the imperfections, sees the dents and smudges, yet still tries to ignore them. Like a photographer, she tries to click snapshots of her dreams, and create in her mind a world, her life, in picture-perfect images. And as she prepares herself for this, she peers into the lens, the tinted windows of her soul, and sees that even that is smeared. So with each passing day, she pretends. I pretend. We pretend. And we continue to live our own truths, mixed with lies and disappointments.

I close my eyes and behind my lids I see shadows moving in the darkness. Before I can make out what they are, sleep claims me. And when I awaken, it is almost eight.

Eight

F our days have passed since my session with Dr. Curtis. I've finished reading the book, *Shattered Souls*, and thoughts of what I want for myself have now begun to take shape and consume me. This book was a wonderfully crafted novel that made me weep at the end. Out of all the characters in the book, I was honestly able to relate to Chyna. Her life felt so similar to mine. Although she wasn't in an abusive marriage, she felt lost, like me. Like her, I feel that despite everything I have, I have nothing. Britton's nonexistent relationship with his abusive father made me wonder about the type of relationship my sons will have with theirs. Will they want nothing to do with him? Will they become just like him? Will they have trouble committing, and loving, and avoid relationships? Will they blame me for staying? Hate me for leaving? These questions begin to weigh heavily on me.

I'm beginning to realize that in my earnest desire to be a loving wife and mother, I have completely abandoned myself. I have failed to pay attention to myself. Instead I have substituted my husband's needs, his wants, and desires, for my own. Besides the running of errands, and the cooking, and the cleaning, and the caretaking, there's nothing more to my life. The realization that I have no identity of my own leaves me feeling light-headed. Dr. Curtis had to have known these characters would come to life in my head, that they'd begin talking to me. He just had to.

Two nights ago, the silence was broken. I am not surprised when he breaks the stillness between us. His need to fill his carnal desires is what brings him to me, eager and ready. Randy cannot go more than a week without sex. And as usual, I don't turn him away. With each thrust, I welcome him back into the space he claims as his own.

As I reflect on my life's journey, tears gather in the corners of my eyes. Behind the verbal put-downs, underneath the blanket threats, I am forced to see things for what they are: subtle—and sometimes, overt—versions of domestic violence. In all honesty, long before the first slap or punch, Randy had masterfully laid the groundwork for violence in our relationship. I just refused to admit it. Dr. Curtis is right. Denial helps me to ignore it. I don't think any woman wants to be abused. And I believe there are a large percentage of women, like me, who truly believe that being in an abusive situation could—would—never happen to them. But I'm realizing it can. And it has.

In the blink of an eye, you can find yourself sucked into a vicious cycle of abuse. As I am slowly learning, when someone hits you, it's easily recognizable, but when you're being verbally abused, when your spirit is being attacked, it goes unchecked, oftentimes undetected, and it's so much more difficult to define, let alone address. Unlike physical abuse, verbal abuse sneaks up on you. As women who love, we refute it or just accept it and become too afraid to do anything about it. Many of us will endure years of unhappiness before we recognize and acknowl-edge there's a problem. Then there are those who will find the strength, will muster the courage, to leave and never look back. Unfortunately, many of us will stay for whatever reason. At least that's how it is for me. I stay, clinging to hope, trying to love my husband with all that's in me, believing things will get better. But I have to wonder if they ever will. Have to wonder if I'll ever get out from under the grip of domestic violence.

I stare at the calendar. It's the fifth of April. It feels like the days are colliding, twisting and turning, getting away from me. I make a mental note to schedule my hair and nail appointments, then go upstairs and luxuriate in a long, hot bubble bath.

At one p.m., Randy calls and says he'll be home late. Says he has a late business meeting. I understand the intent of his call, knowing that it isn't out of courtesy. But I appreciate the gesture nonetheless. Still, a part of me is relieved. I am happy to not have to race around to prepare a meal he may not want to eat. I decide I will not slave over a stove. Not today. I will order out. I will not dirty up dishes. We will eat on paper plates for a change. I will put the triplets to bed early, then curl up on my chaise, close my door, and read undisturbed. This is what I have decided I want for me, for now.

The phone rings for the fourth time. Each time it's Randy with something he wants—no, needs—me to take care of: Take his shirts to the cleaners. Pick up his watch from the jeweler. Make sure I take the car to get the tires rotated. All the things he can do on Saturday, he expects me to do. "Today," he says, before hanging up. I let his demands linger, then fade. My mind is already made up. Today, I'm doing nothing. And I'm prepared to deal with the tantrum that will surely come.

I fix myself something to eat, pour a glass of mineral water, slice a lemon and squeeze its juice in, then pull a stool out from under the breakfast nook and sit. Flipping through my latest issue of *Essence*, I take one forkful of my tuna salad when the phone rings. I ignore its sound for a moment, pulling in a deep breath. After the sixth ring, I glance at the screen. I am thankful when the number that flashes isn't Randy's.

"Hello," I answer.

"Hey, girl," Janie says. Her voice sounds strained and it catches me by surprise.

"Hey," I say back. "Is everything all right?"

"Simone is pregnant," she blurts out. "And she had the gall to tell me she's keeping it and that there was nothing I could say to stop her."

I am shocked. "Pregnant?" I repeat.

"You heard me. The girl is knocked up and wants to keep it. What in the world is she going to do with a baby at her age? I don't know how many times I have told her to always use a condom. I have said it over and over, until I was almost blue in the face. Protect yourself. I even made sure she was on the pill to keep something like this from happening because I know you can't stop these teens from having sex nowadays. But protect yourself. Not just from pregnancy, but from STDs as well. That's what I've asked of her. And what does she do? She goes and gets herself pregnant anyway. Just being defiant and hardheaded.

"And if that's not the icing on the cake, she tells me she wanted to get pregnant. That she was grown and that she was capable of making her own decisions. Girlfriend put her hands up on her narrow hips and told me she was sick and tired of me trying to control her life and that she was moving in with his family. I told her over my dead body." I try to keep up, but she's talking a mile a minute. "I tried to slap her face off, talking to me like that. If it wasn't for the fact that we were still in the parking lot of the doctor's office, I would have beat her senseless." She takes a breath.

Oh my goodness, I think. I have never known Janie to raise a hand to either of her children or talk of physical disciplining. Time-outs and punishments are the only things used in her home. "When did you find out?"

"Two days ago. Last week I dreamt of fish three nights in a row, and knew someone was pregnant. And it sure wasn't me. Then Mom called me and said she had had the same dream. Of course we both thought it was you, *again*." My brow raises. I want to confront her on what that was supposed to mean but decide against it. She continues. "Then it dawned on me that I didn't recall Simone having her period this month. Hers usually comes a few days after mine. So I confronted her. Of course she hemmed and hawed, and shifted her eyes every which way. So I made an appointment and took her behind to the doctor's."

"How many months is she?" I ask.

"Nearly two," she states.

Suddenly my stomach knots with anxiety for my niece. "And how old is he?"

"Almost nineteen, and doesn't have a pot to piss in, or a window to throw it out of. The boy doesn't even have a decent job. I'm so disgusted I don't know what to do. The last thing I need is to become the talk of the Beach Club gossip mill. She knows better than this. Girl, if I thought I could get away with beating it out of her I would. This is not the life I wanted for her."

It becomes clear. This isn't really about Simone being pregnant. It's the idea that Janie's family's image will be tarnished, that her world won't be seen as flawless before the watchful eyes of her neatly coiffed, freshly made-up, high-society associates, acquaintances, and so-called friends. Sadly, a part of me understands this need for perfection, for different reasons, of course. "How is Rodney taking this?" I decide to ask.

She lets out a heavy sigh. "Ugh, don't even get me started. Our child's whole life is down the drain and he's as calm as the day is long, telling me to relax. Says we'll handle it. Of course he thinks I'm being overly dramatic."

"Hmm," I say. "Well, have you spoken to this young man's family?"

"Yeah. Yesterday. Not that it did any good. His ghetto-fabulous mother came to the door with a mouth full of teeth trimmed in gold, looking more like his sister, wearing all this loud makeup and this way-too-small mini-dress and a pair of hooker pumps like she was ready for a night on the ho-stroll. I'm telling you, she is a real ghetto queen. And these are the kind of people Simone wants to associate with. Low budget, and classless."

I'm not sure why, but today I'm offended by Janie's uppishness. We were raised to be tolerant of everyone, regardless of his or her socio-economic background. But it's apparent she has forgotten her upbringing.

"Well, what did she have to say about all of this?"

"Girlfriend said her son was 'fucking grown' and could do whatever he wanted. If he's man enough to make a baby, he's man enough to raise it because she wasn't taking care of no more babies 'cause she had four of her own. Then she had the nerve to tell me I should be glad that her son wanted to take care of his responsibilities and be a father since he didn't know his own. And, are you ready for the clincher?" she asks, pausing.

"I'm almost scared to know," I say.

"This hoochie-mama had the nerve to say she would help Simone go down to Social Services so she could apply for W.I.C. and Medicaid."

"Get out. No she didn't!" I exclaim.

"Oh, yes she did. I almost passed out. What kind of madness is that?"

"And what did you say to that?"

"I told her if that was the kind of life she lived, fine. But my child would not be a part of that way of living. Not if I had anything to do about it. She had the nerve to laugh in my face, then started rolling her neck at me and told me to take my stuck-up, high-yellow ass back across town before she fucked me up. She slammed the door in my face. I was too through. I couldn't believe her. I turned on my heels, got in my car, and sped off."

I try to replay the scene in my mind, shaking my head. The thought of seeing Janie all dolled up in her expensive attire, being proper and ladylike while this woman has her hand on her hip, rolling her neck, and cursing is...priceless. I almost chuckle, but catch myself. "You and Rodney have raised Simone with good values and morals. So hopefully she'll make the right decision."

"Well, until she does," she says, "there's no car, no cell, no TV, no computer, no stereo, no allowance. No more weekly manicures and pedicures and facials. No more running to get her hair done. Nothing. Since she's so darn grown."

I glance at the clock. It is almost three p.m. K'wan and Kyle will be home soon. I allow Janie to vent for five more minutes, then tell her I'll call her back. When I hang up, her words, "we thought it was you *again*," loiter in my thoughts. Frantically, I search my Rolodex for my gynecologist's number and make an appointment. Just in case.

When Randy gets home, it is a little after nine. I am sitting in the family room. Teena Marie's *Sapphire* CD fills the room and I'm reading "Victory Begins with Me" in the *Breaking the Cycle* anthology. I feel his eyes on me. I know he's there without looking up and can already tell he's in one of his moods before he opens his mouth. I look up from my book to gauge his attitude.

I offer a smile. "Hey, how was your day?" I ask, laying my book facedown beside me.

"It was all right," he says, stepping into the room. "So, what'd you do today?"

"Not much," I offer.

"Hmm." He purses his lips, a sign of what's coming next. And I'm prepared to respond. "Did you do any of the things I asked you to do today?"

"No. I didn't," I say calmly.

"And why not?" he asks incredulously.

"Because I didn't feel like running errands today," I say, hoping my tone isn't confrontational.

"What do you mean *you* didn't *feel* like running errands today?"

I shrug. "I just didn't."

He eyes me. "Did you at least cook?"

I shake my head. "We ordered in."

Silence.

"So, once again, you sat around on your fat behind all day doing nothing?"

I tilt my head. Let the sting of his dig subside. "No, Randy. I have been up since six o'clock this morning, as I am every morning, making breakfast for the boys. Then, in between taking care of three sick, cranky toddlers, I gave myself a facial, took a long hot bath, read, and listened to music. When the boys got in from school, I helped them with their homework, made sure everyone ate, had playtime with the triplets, gave them their baths, then put them to bed. And as you can see, the house is quiet and clean as it always is." I pause, allow what I say to linger as he glares at me. "So I'd say that my *fat* behind, as you call it, was doing a lot for one day."

The muscles in his face twitch. His fists open and close at his sides, tightening into balls of fury. He takes a step toward me, but stops himself. He throws his hands up. "Whatever," he snaps. "I'm going to take a shower."

"Enjoy," I say in a whisper, picking up my book and burying my face back into its pages.

He charges toward me. "What did you just say?" He snatches the book from out of my hands, slinging it across the room.

I flinch. "I *said* I'll be up in a minute," I lie to avoid a physical confrontation.

"Ever since you started going to that shrink of yours, you've been getting real mouthy."

"No, Randy," I say. "I'm just slowly starting to see life through a different set of eyes." It is too late to take back what I have said. I am shocked by my own brazenness.

He steps in closer, points his finger in my face. I jerk my head back. His finger is practically touching the space between my eyes. "I'm telling you right now," he snaps. "I'm not in the mood for your damn mouth. You say one more thing, and I'm gonna shove something down it. Do you understand me?" His eyes have become narrow slits. His right hand opens and closes into a tight fist. I am sure he is going to hit me. I know the next thing I say—if it's not to his liking—will be the spark that sets him off.

"Yes, Randy," I concede, looking up at him. "I understand."

He glares at me, then storms out, fuming.

I let out a soft, relieved sigh. He will let me be for the moment. But in the back of my mind I am keenly aware that although this discussion is over, I will have to ready myself for the repercussions that may or may not follow.

I get up to retrieve the book that I have become engrossed in, then plop back down on the sofa. *Victory definitely begins with me*, I think, losing myself in the last few pages of the story. When I am done, I lay my head back and close my eyes, feeling overwhelmed by the overall theme of the book. The harsh realities of each story have hit too close to home. Getting up, I decide I have read enough for one night. I shut off the lights and go upstairs. I check in on the boys, then make my way to my bedroom. I am glad Randy is already deep in sleep. His light snore ripples through the room. I shower, slip on a nightgown, then slide into my side of the bed. I lie on my back staring into darkness, waiting for sleep to come.

❖❖❖

I am sleepy, but can't seem to doze off. Shutting my eyes, I try to force sleep. But I am too wound up. The house is quiet. Randy is beside me, oblivious to the gnawing pain in the pit of my soul. His snores come in spurts, breaking the silence that has muted the room. I snatch a glance over at him, then at the clock. It's three a.m. I have been lying here for three hours, staring at the ceiling, feeling like my world has been put on pause, and there's a part of me that's not breathing. I feel as if I am slowly dying. And I wonder if it's too late. I am struggling to resuscitate that piece of my life—the life I'd given up for the sake of loving someone who hasn't always been good at respecting me, at loving me back in the same regard. But I don't know how.

Something forces my thoughts to drift back, eight months ago. Long before my call to Dr. Curtis, before I was willing to acknowledge there was a problem—the day I felt so down and out that, in my desperate attempt to find an escape, I contemplated taking my own life. The realization that my "perfect" life wasn't faultless, that my ideal world was spiraling out of control had caused me to believe that suicide was the answer.

K'wan was out bike riding with a few of his friends from the neighborhood when a drunk driver's car swerved up on the sidewalk and hit him. He was knocked off his bike and suffered a concussion and broken arm. Randy blamed me. He yelled and screamed, and called me an unfit mother.

"You don't have to do anything but stay home and sit on your sloppy ass and take care of my kids and you can't even do that right. What good are you? I pay all the bills. Make sure you have everything you want. And you can't even pay attention to what's going on around here. He could have been killed. You're so fucking worthless!"

I was stunned that he had called me a *sloppy ass*. *Worthless*. And hurt that he actually blamed me for what had happened. Feeling attacked, I tried to defend myself but he said I was making excuses for my carelessness. Although he later apologized, blaming his behavior on being upset, the damage had already been done. He said what he felt. My guilt had me believing him.

Two days later, feeling as though I had failed at being a good mother, that somehow it really was my fault, that somehow I was neglectful and of no value to my family, believing that they'd be better off without me, I picked up my car keys, walked out to the garage, got into my SUV, and turned the engine on. I sat behind the wheel, closed my eyes and embraced my fate. As tears fell, images of my sons' faces kept flashing in my head. And the sobs became uncontrollable. The thought of one of them finding my limp body, and how that would affect them for the rest of their lives forced me to turn off the ignition. I sat behind the wheel, screaming and crying like a madwoman, banging on the steering wheel and the dashboard. I knew then I was losing it. But denial kept me believing things would get better. It still does.

❖❖❖

Randy's coughing startles me, and brings me back to the present. My memories cause fresh tears to escape my eyes. Hurt resurfaces. Although I know it's my imagination, I taste blood. I feel the swelling, the heaviness of my husband's fist against my face. In flashes, I see and hear his violent attacks against me. Slowly, pain finds every part of me. I wince. Close my eyes. Lie still as stone and will the pounding in my mind to stop. When the thumping finally subsides, I quietly climb out of bed and tiptoe over to my walk-in closet. I turn on the light and close the door, shutting myself out from the pain that follows behind me. I open my great-grandmother's hope chest. It is a gift my grandmother had given me before she died. The crisp smell of cedar greets me and a faint smile forms on my lips. Any time I open her chest it takes me back to fond memories of her. The recollections create wonderful feelings in me.

Finally, I retrieve what I'm looking for. My journal. Buried deep in the bottom, tucked in a box beneath layers of old sweaters and memories: photos of my youth along with high school and college yearbooks and memorabilia. My fingers trail the edges of my journal. I stare at it for a moment, then slip into my sitting room and sit in my chaise, flipping through it. The pages are mostly blank. Sheets of emptiness, like my life. *What does Syreeta want for Syreeta?*

I stare out of the huge window overlooking our neatly manicured lawn, into filtered darkness. Emotionally, I am unbalanced. The scale tips. Guilt and fear and uncertainty weigh me down. Mentally, I am unfocused. Denial and love and hope blind me. Why, Lord? I ask. What am I to do? Where do I begin?

I press my eyes closed, take in a deep breath. I wait. And I wait. And I wait. Hoping balance and perspective find its way to me. What do I want for me? I play the question in my head over and over. Then, in the wee hours of the morning, against the clutter of my own internal conflict, the answer comes to me in an avalanche of bold, bright colors. Words find me. And I do something I haven't done in years. I write:

Shattered Soul

Breathlessly,
I looked in the mirror
And saw the reflection of a past

And present
I've tried to forget
Misery
Loneliness
Confusion
Clawing
And
Gnawing
At the heart of lost dreams
Stolen promises
And
Misplaced trust

Memories that live
And breathe
And beat
Within the clutter
Of sadness
Haunt me

Beaten
And
Worn
A face of abandonment
And contempt
Scarred by disappointment
Streaked by pain

A walking shell
Broken
And discarded

Soiled by hands
That fondled
And bruised me

An empty vessel
Dampened by a tongue
That disrespected me
Starved me
Neglected me
And robbed me of emotions
Causing my blood to run cold
And form blisters on my spirit
That now bleeds with agony

Choking
Gasping
Suffocating
Pleading
As I drown in my own tears
Frightened by the image standing before me
Unsure of the future
I ask God
To make me whole
To help me put back together
The scattered pieces of my life
And mend my shattered soul.

When I am done, I close my journal, clutch it against my aching heart, and cry.

Nine

I am happy it is Thursday. I want to talk. Need to release things I've kept burrowed under a blanket of sadness. I anticipate the discussion I will have with Dr. Curtis about the books he has asked me to read.

"Syreeta, how are you today?" he asks, sitting in his usual seat across from me.

I sigh. "I'm okay, I guess."

He opens his folder and nods. "Have you had a chance to read the books I gave you?"

I nod, reaching in my satchel and pulling them out. "I finished them both the other night," I say, placing them on the table.

"Oh, no," he says, lifting his hands to stop me. "Those are for you. I want you to keep them."

"Are you sure?" I ask, surprised.

"Yes. The author of *Shattered Souls* is a good friend of mine. I know he'd want you to have it."

I feel honored. "Wow. Thank you," I say, reaching for the books, then placing them back in my bag.

"No problem. So, what did you think of them?" he asks, leaning back in his seat.

"I really enjoyed them. I thought they were both very thought-provoking. It just goes to show you really can't judge a book by its cover. What a person seems like on the outside isn't always who they really are on the inside. And unless you've walked in their shoes, you can never fully understand their pain or the choices they've made. I can honestly say both books evoked a range of emotions in me."

He smiles knowingly. "You're right. Most people who read them say the same thing; that's why I give them out." We spend the next ten minutes discussing how each book affected me, particularly *Shattered Souls*. How I laughed and cried, and wanted to scream one minute, then cheered the characters on the next. How I had awakened up in the middle of the night and started writing in my journal.

"Hmm…that's great. Writing can be very good for the soul. One day, I'd like to see what you've written."

I smile. "Sure. I'd like that."

"Good," he says, closing my file and letting it rest in his lap. "Today, I was hoping we could switch gears a little, if that's all right with you."

I shrug. "I guess. What did you have in mind?"

"Let's talk a little about your childhood," he says.

"Umm…what would you like to know?" I ask, shifting in my seat.

"Tell me about your family. Are your parents alive? Do you have any siblings?"

"My mother is," I answer. "My father died ten years ago. And I have an older sister who is married with two children." I tell him about her prosperous career and her memberships in various organizations.

"You and your sister sound like night and day. Are the two of you close?"

"For the most part we are."

"Just traveling different paths," he offers.

"Basically," I say. A feeling of sadness slowly sweeps over me. I try to shift my thoughts, knowing tears will surface if I reflect too long. Unfortunately, my mind races in a hundred directions at once, chasing memories of my childhood: how my mother basically ignored me growing up, constantly doting over Janie. They cut through me like a knife. How she always found a way to compare me to her, and remind me that I wasn't as smart, or as pretty. How I always felt I needed to compete for her love, attention, and most importantly her approval. And somehow, no matter what I did, I still managed to come up short. Growing up in the shadow of Janie had been stressful for me. Even in school, as soon as teachers learned that I was her sister, they'd comment on how popular, smart, and pretty she was. How she excelled academically in all of her honors classes. How she was voted most popular, and most likely to succeed in her senior year. All of the accolades and praise she received chipped at my self-esteem. Although we shared similiar physical features, I wasn't as graceful and charming as she was. I wasn't active in organizations. I wasn't outgoing. I wasn't anything like my sister. And no one was able to accept me for who I was. No one seemed capable of seeing the beauty in me—no one except Randy. My gaze alternates between Dr. Curtis and my folded hands in my lap.

"What about you and your mother?" he asks thoughtfully.

I look up at him and force a smile that I hope he doesn't recognize as another mask I wear, one covering the emptiness that hides among the crevices of my soul. I think about his question for a moment, not wanting to say the wrong thing. "I love her," I finally say, "if that's what you're asking. But growing up, I always felt like she favored my sister over me." No sooner had I said this I wished I could take it back. The look in Dr. Curtis's eyes tells me he wants to know more. I hope I am wrong. I do not want to pick at the scabs of old wounds, not today.

"How so?"

I knew it. I purse my lips, quickly searching for a sanitized version to share. "I guess because Janie was so rebellious, very headstrong, and determined to do whatever she wanted, however she wanted. She was extremely outspoken, very opinionated, and seemed to take up a lot of my mother's time and attention; where I was very quiet, shy, and more reserved. I was compliant. I followed all of the rules, never talked back. Did what was expected of me without complaint."

"Do you envy your sister for that?"

"Not at all," I say, hoping it sounds convincing. But, the truth is I have always admired Janie for having those qualities. I am sure if I had more of her personality I might not have made the same choices. Perhaps my life would be different.

"You know it's not uncommon for siblings to love each other, yet be envious and, oftentimes, jealous of each other."

"Jealous!" It is almost a question. But in my heart, I already know the answer. Still, I refuse to admit it. "Not at all," I state incredulously. "And I'm sure Janie is far from jealous of me. She has no reason to be."

"Are you sure of that?"

"Of course I am. Why, do you think I am?"

"Only you can answer that," he says. "But it wouldn't surprise me. After all, she seems to represent all of the things you have always wanted to be. And she seems to have the one thing you have always wanted."

"And what's that?" I ask, almost afraid to hear his response. "The courage to stand up for herself, and be her own woman." What he says knocks the wind out of me. I don't expect him to say that. Don't expect him to be so direct. There is so much truth to his words that it stings. I pull in a deep breath. He must sense how hurt I am, and immediately offers a soothing blanket of comfort.

"Syreeta, beneath your bruises is a beautiful woman who will heal, a woman who will one day find her voice and make her own decisions. You just have to trust in your strengths, and believe that change is going to come. That you are deserving of something much more than the pain you have endured. One day the hollowness in the pit of your soul will fill with happiness, joy, and peace."

He has touched me, found that space that aches, and I begin to cry. He patiently allows silence and my emotions to fill the hole between us. When I am done, I wipe my eyes with the back of my hands, then pull a handful of tissues out of my purse to wipe my face, blow my nose.

"I'm so sorry," I say, catching my breath.

"No need to apologize. I am here to help you. No matter how long the journey. Besides, crying cleanses the soul." He offers me a warm, comforting smile.

Despite myself, a faint smile creeps on my face. "Thank you."

"No thanks needed; it comes with the territory. So, would you like to continue or would you rather we stopped here?"

I shake my head. "No, please. I'd like to finish up, if that's okay with you."

He nods, then picks up his pad. "So, tell me about your father. Were you close to him at all?"

I slowly shake my head. "Not really. I mean...I loved him. And I know he loved me. But he didn't really show it often. He provided for us financially. We wanted for nothing, but emotionally he was sometimes distant. My mother always said it was because he was too tired from all the long hours he put in at work."

"Do you believe that?"

"I guess," I say. "He was a hardworking man."

"What kind of work did he do?" Dr. Curtis asks.

"He owned his own trucking company."

"And your mother, did she work?"

"No. She was a homemaker."

"Sounds like you were brought up in a rather traditional household. Dad worked, mom stayed home, raised the kids, and managed the house."

I shrug. "I suppose. I mean, I never really gave it much thought. My mother felt that it was her duty to be a stay-at-home mom and wife. And I guess that's what my father expected of her. It seemed to work for them. My father believed family should come before anything else. That it was a man's responsibility to be the breadwinner and a woman's duty to make sure the family was taken care of. And my mother supported that belief."

"Is that how you were raised?"

I nod. "Yes. We were raised to believe that the man rules the house, and that you don't contradict him no matter how you may feel about it."

In my mind's eye, I see my mother cooking and ironing and cleaning, always picking up behind my father. Always agreeing to whatever he wanted or said. Never confronting him; never

challenging his authority. My mother was content being a housewife. A good wife and mother was all she aspired to be. I shake
my head, thinking about Janie and her marriage. How vocal she
is. How ambitious and independent she is. "Obviously," I say
forlornly, "out of the two of us, I'm the one that it stuck with."

"Do you agree with that belief system?"

"A part of me does," I reply. "But then there's a part of me
that believes a woman should have a choice as to whether or
not she wants to stay home. And she should be allowed to have
her own opinions about how things should be without seeming
like she's trying to challenge her mate, or being confrontational."

"Do you feel you were given a choice?"

For some reason, I am starting to feel cornered. But I answer
anyway. "Not really," I say. I sense he wants me to elaborate on
my feelings. But I don't know if I can.

"Sounds like you've carried some of those beliefs with you."

"I suppose, subconsciously," I admit, "I have tried to be…"—
the words catch in my throat—"in some ways, I guess I am…
like my mother."

"And Randy sounds a bit like your father," Dr. Curtis offers.

I am not sure if I am ready to agree with that observation.
"Not really. I mean, my father never raised his voice, nor did we
ever hear him talk down to our mother. And as far as I know, he
never hit her."

"But you felt he was emotionally distant?"

I nod. "Sometimes."

"Then for argument's sake," he says, gauging my reaction,
"your father was a good provider, hardworking, and a man of
principle?"

I nod cautiously, trying to figure out where he is going with this. He explains how some psychologists suggest women tend to look for the qualities of their fathers in their mates. That they are often attracted to men who tend to be just like their fathers, or at best have similar traits that remind her of him, both good and bad.

"I never really thought of it like that," I say, tilting my head.

"It's like the little girl within," he says, folding his hands, "waits in vain for the moment when her father will fill the empty spaces in her life with the love and attention she's always wanted from him. But when he doesn't, she seeks out men who she believes can. Men who she thinks can replace him. And that sometimes can be very painful. Because she ends up getting hurt, being disappointed, becoming disillusioned, and feeling let down all over again."

Tears begin to fill my eyes again. "Is that what you think I've done?" I ask, trying to keep my emotions in check.

"What do you think?"

"I don't know."

"Well, it's definitely something to consider. The biggest issue for most women is dealing with abandonment from emotionally withdrawn or absent fathers. Let me ask you something. What did your father think of your husband?"

"He liked him a lot," I answer.

"And your mother and sister?"

"My mother thinks he's the greatest man alive. And Janie... well, she hasn't said one way or the other how she really feels about him. She just wants me to be happy."

"Do they know about the abuse?"

I shake my head. "No."

"Why?"

I turn away from his gaze. I think back to three years ago, revisiting a conversation with my mother a few months after the triplets were born. She had come up to visit. Prior to her coming, Randy and I had had a huge fight about her wanting to stay for a month. He said his parents were coming up around the same time, yet he never mentioned anything to me about it until after I told him of my mother's plans. When I told him this, he accused me of calling him a liar. The argument escalated and he tossed his glass of water in my face, then stormed out of the room, leaving me feeling mortified.

"Where's my wonderful son-in-law?" my mother had asked. We were sitting out on the deck, drinking white tea. Her favorite. "I haven't seen him all day."

I forced a smile. "He left early for the office, and probably won't be home until late this evening."

She smiled, taking a slow sip. "I hope you realize how lucky you are to have a man like Randall," she replied, eyeing me over the rim of her cup. "He's every woman's dream."

"Mom, sometimes I don't feel so lucky," I confided.

She knitted her brow. "What do you mean?"

I shrugged. "Sometimes he talks down to me. He can be nasty. And he makes me feel unloved. The other night, he actually threw a glass of ice water in my face."

She pursed her lips. "Has he hit you?" she asked, her tone dismissive.

I nodded. "Once."

"Well, what did you do to upset him?" she asked.

"Nothing," I said incredulously.

"Are you sure?"

"Of course I am," I stated, offended. I had expected a tender, motherly gesture, a warm embrace or some comforting words. Not insinuations that perhaps it was something that I might have done for him to humiliate me. "I've done nothing but be a good wife and mother."

I tried to keep my feelings in check. But a wave of sadness began to overwhelm me. And tears fell from my eyes.

She got up from her seat, held my face between her hands and looked me in the eyes. "Stop all this foolishness. What the devil is wrong with you? Look around you. You have a beautiful home, healthy children, and a husband who takes excellent care of his family. You and the boys want for nothing. Randall is a good, decent man. You just need to stop looking for problems and be grateful for what you have. One slap is nothing to be crying over. There are women out here who would love to be in your shoes."

I glanced up at her, feeling the heaviness of my heart in my chest. I wished I had never shared that with her. I knew then, we'd never be able to have this conversation again. She was on his side. And whatever happened between Randy and me would always, somehow, be my fault.

No. Sharing with my mother, or my sister for that matter, was not an option.

A tear escapes my eye. I wipe it before it can make its journey down my cheek. "I don't want to burden them," I say softly, returning my gaze to Dr. Curtis.

He stares at me. "You don't think they'd be supportive?"

I shake my head. "They'd never understand."

He nods knowingly. "How would you describe your parents' relationship growing up?"

I consider the question, lean my head back against the sofa, then close my eyes and search through my mental Rolodex for memories. "My father rarely raised his voice, but when he did, you knew it was serious. I suppose they loved each other. Yet their relationship seemed... routine. He worked, paid the bills. And my mother took care of everything else. I don't ever really remember them being affectionate toward each other in front of us. Can't remember him ever walking in from work and kissing her, or asking her how her day was. Just giving orders and asking her if she took care of whatever he had left for her to do for the day. And she'd always nod and say, 'Yes dear.' She could be dog-tired or sick and she'd still drag herself out of bed every morning to lay his clothes out for work, make his breakfast, pack his lunch, and did anything else he wanted or needed done."

"How did your father die?" he asks.

I think back on the day he died. Remember the pain in my mother's voice, feel her tears. He had come home early from work, stating he wasn't feeling well, something he never did. He had told her he was going to take a shower, then lie down, and for her to wake him when dinner was ready. Four hours later, when she went upstairs to get him, she found him lying on the bathroom floor. There was no pulse. She called 911 and attempted CPR. But she was unable to resuscitate him. He was forty-seven. He died six months before my wedding.

"Heart attack," I say softly.

"Sorry to hear that," Dr. Curtis replies thoughtfully.

"Thank you."

"Is there anything you wish you could have said to him, or would have liked to hear from him, before he died?"

I feel a lump forming in my throat. I swallow hard, close my eyes, and hold back the tears I feel swelling behind my lids. Not a day has gone by that I haven't thought about him. I return my gaze to Dr. Curtis, wiping my eyes. "That I loved him. And to hear that he loved me back."

Dr. Curtis smiles, then glances at his watch. I know without him saying it. The extra thirty minutes he has allowed me is up. I leave his office, wondering if what he has said is true. That Randy is like my father. Wondering when my voice will come. Wondering if I will ever breathe again.

Ten

Randy has come home early today. He is standing in the doorway holding a long white box wrapped with a big red bow. "I hope you haven't started dinner," he says, gliding into the den where I am sitting, reading.

I glance at my watch. It is one o'clock. "No, not yet," I say, laying my book facedown and looking up at him. He is wearing a wide smile. One I haven't seen in months. "Is there something special you want?"

He walks over to me and plants a soft, warm kiss on my lips. "Yeah, I want to take my lovely wife, the mother of my handsome sons, into the city. I've made reservations at the Four Seasons for dinner, and reserved a suite for us at the hotel." He tells me his sister will pick up the boys from their schools and will watch them overnight while we paint the town. I am at a loss for words. We haven't spent any quality time together, alone, in almost a year. He hands me the box. "These are for you."

"What's this?" I ask, surprised.

"Open it." He sits beside me, resting his hand on my thigh, waiting for me to untie the box and open it. I oblige him, and smile. It's filled with two dozen long-stemmed roses.

"They're beautiful," I say, lifting them to my nose and inhaling their fragrance. "Thank you."

"Not as beautiful as you," he says, planting another kiss on my lips. I am completely taken off guard by this thoughtful act. He must sense this. "I know I don't always tell you, or show you, how much I love you. But you're my world. Hope you know that." I look into his eyes and smile faintly. For the first time in a very long time there is something warm, inviting, in the way he is looking at me. The sparkle in his eyes causes me to feel a rush I haven't felt in a long time, the way it did the first time I laid eyes on him. Can we ever recapture what we once shared? It is a question I am not sure I want answered. Somehow, somewhere, buried deep within the core of my being, I know we most likely can't. But, I still wish.

As I wonder where this Randy, the man I married and put my faith in, has been hiding, reservations rise in me. For months, I have felt as if my spirit has been uprooted and is withering. And, today, he sits before me offering seeds of promise, wanting to harvest a new beginning. I swallow, trying to dislodge the lump that forms in my throat. "I love you, too," I say softly in a voice unknown to me. And that frightens me.

"I know you do," he states, pulling me into his arms, then kissing me on the head. I crane my neck and look up at him, hoping my skepticism doesn't show on my face. I don't want to say the wrong thing, or think the wrong thoughts, but uncertainty becomes a swirling current in my head. To keep myself from messing up the mood, I smile and try to accept the moment for what it is. A start.

I nestle into him. "I know things between us have been a bit strained," he continues. "And I've been a little edgy lately. It's just that I've been so stressed with work. But I promise you, as soon as this quarter is over, I'm gonna make it up to you and the boys."

"I understand," I offer. I say this, not really sure if I do or not. But I allow the words to leave my lips nonetheless.

"I've been thinking maybe we should go to counseling, together" he suggests as he strokes the side of my face. I raise up, look him in the eyes, surprised.

"Counseling?" I repeat.

"Yeah. You know, just for a few sessions to help us get back on track. You and the boys are my life. The thought of you trying to leave me makes me crazy. I'd lose my mind without you, baby." He says this with a conviction that shakes me, sends a chill down my spine. I try to ignore the nagging sense of urgency, the sound of desperation in his tone. I don't know how to respond. Instead, I kiss his lips, and allow him to wrap me in his arms. However, even in his embrace, there's an unsettling feeling I am unable to explain, like there is something unknown or unseen lurking in the shadows, waiting to strike. I am afraid to trust what I want so badly to feel in my heart, that this is a sign that things between Randy and me will get better. Sadly, I don't know what to think, or believe. But what I do know is that my husband is extremely unpredictable. And I am walking a tightrope of hope. The question is: If I open my eyes and look down, how far will I fall?

Eleven

W e have reservations for the Pool Room at the Four Seasons restaurant. The ambiance is soothing and romantic with its gurgling marble pool. I smile, as Randy takes me by the hand and we follow the maître d' to our table. Once we're seated, he orders a bottle of Veuve Clicquot.

"You're so beautiful," he says, gazing at me. My husband is full of compliments and affection tonight. He says all the right things to smooth the edges of my doubt. On the ride into the city, he reached over, took my hand in his, and held it while driving, alternating between kissing my hand and telling me how much he loves me, how thankful he is to have me in his life, how wonderful a mother I am to his children. Something he hasn't done in years. The flicker of lust in Randy's eyes causes an unexpected flutter of nervousness. This side of my husband has become foreign to me. Yet, it somehow excites me. I wonder if he realizes his effect on me, if he truly understands his hold on me. I feel like a love-struck schoolgirl on her first date. I blush in spite of my best efforts not to.

"Thank you," I say, matching his smile.

When the waiter returns, he presents our bottle of champagne, then pours the chilled bubbly into two glasses. I feel myself getting lightheaded as a string of bubbles float to the top. He hands us our flutes, then takes our orders. Randy orders a butternut salad and the Dover sole. I order a spinach salad with grilled salmon. When the waiter leaves, Randy raises his glass. "To us."

"To us," I repeat, clinking the lip of my flute with his, then taking a slow sip.

Randy takes a sip as well, then rests his glass on the table. "Before I forget, I have something for you." I give him a surprised look. He reaches into his suit jacket and pulls out a long, narrow, Tiffany box. "Syreeta, baby," he says, handing it to me, "you are my lifeline. Like the air I breathe, and the beat of my heart, I need you. Without you, I am nothing. I am my beloved's, and my beloved is mine."

The man sitting before me speaking does not sound like the distant, detached Randy I've come to know over the years. He looks like him, and feels like him. But there's something very different about the man in front of me. He sounds like someone who romanticizes and embraces love, someone who adores his wife and children. He sounds like someone who enjoys, and lives, and appreciates life. I am not exactly sure who this stranger is in front of me. I am afraid to trust him. Yet, his words touch me. Make me want to stamp this moment into my memory. The Randy here with me tonight makes me wonder if we'll find our way back to where we once were—happy. This Randy keeps me loving him, and wanting him, in spite of his capriciousness.

I open the box and gasp. Inside is a platinum and diamond tennis bracelet. "It's exquisite," I say, lifting it from its box.

"But not as lovely as you," he says, taking the bracelet from me, and holding my gaze. I extend my arm as he fastens the clasp. "Just a little something to show you how much I appreciate you."

I hold the bracelet up and admire it. "Thank you. I'm speechless. First, the lovely flowers, dinner, and now this. I don't know what else to say. It's breathtaking."

He smiles. "I don't want you to say anything. Tonight, I only want you to know just how much I love you."

I return the smile, genuinely touched.

Throughout dinner, we steal glances at each other, smiling and flirting. The atmosphere, the champagne, the surprise of the moment has me mentally and sexually aroused. Tonight, I want and need the Randy before me to make slow, deep, passionate love to me. I need to feel special; yearn to feel the depth of his love, even if it means closing my eyes and pretending that this is how it will always be.

I am afraid for the night to end. Frightened of what tomorrow will bring. "This has been a lovely evening," I say, reaching over and touching Randy's hand. I stroke it. "Thank you."

"The best is yet to come," he says, taking my hand, then brushing his lips into my palm. He flags our waiter for the check. "Let's get out of here. I can't wait to get you to our suite to make love to you." He gets up from his seat, leans over, and kisses me softly on the lips, oblivious to the smiling glances upon us. A spark of desire ignites a fire inside of me. And for the first time in a very long time, the look in my eyes matches the hunger in his.

❖❖❖

On our way home, the next day, I think back on the events that took place the night before. How Randy had set the stage for an unforgettable evening. He had a Park View Tower Room overlooking Central Park reserved at the Four Seasons Hotel. The view was breathtaking. His kisses were passionate, his touch gentle, his embrace filled with tenderness. With soft music and a candlelit room, Randy—for the first time in years—made slow, sweet, purposeful love to me. And I felt reconnected to him. It almost felt perfect, almost felt right. But there's an urgent nagging in the pit of my soul that warns me that all I feel, that everything I hope for, is just another illusion. And that I should proceed with caution.

My reverie is broken by the sound of Randy's voice. "When we get back to the house," he says, glancing at me. "I want you to call the boys' school and let them know they'll be out for the rest of the week." I look at him, confused. Before I can speak, he continues, "I've booked flights for us to go to Disney World for five days. We're leaving tomorrow."

"Disney World?" I ask. "When did you do that?"

"Before I left the office yesterday," he says matter-of-factly.

We're leaving tomorrow. I am certain I hadn't heard him right. "When did you say we were leaving?"

"Tomorrow," he says.

"Tomorrow," I repeat. "Randy, I can't leave tomorrow. I have my appointment with Doctor Curtis."

"So you mean to tell me you'd rather go to your appointment than go away with your family. Is that what you're telling me?" His brow furrows for emphasis.

I am cornered. "No, of course that's not what I'm saying. It's just that…well, I wasn't expecting this."

"Uh," he says, offering a slight smile dripped with sarcasm. "It's called a surprise. So don't try to ruin it with a bunch of excuses. Call and cancel your appointment. I'm sure the good doctor won't mind if you miss one session."

"I know but…it's so last minute. I have a thousand and one things to do. I need time to get the boys' things together and…"

Randy narrows his eyes. His jaw muscles tighten, then relax. "Syreeta, stop it, okay? We're leaving tomorrow and that's it."

His tone is final. I sense his growing frustration. I quickly remember my place, and know it's best not to push the issue.

"You're right," I say. "I'm sorry. You're just really full of surprises all of a sudden. What's brought all this on?"

His mood softens. "Nothing really," he says, quickly glancing back over at me. "We haven't been anywhere in years, at least not since the triplets were born. I think the getaway would do us all some good."

I try to remember the last time we have done something as a family. He is right. It has been years. Our last family trip was to San Diego almost four years ago, right after we learned I was carrying triplets. Despite my anxiety about being pregnant again, it had turned out to be a very enjoyable trip for us all.

"The boys will be excited," I say, trying to sound eager.

"And what about you?"

I wish you had waited until the end of the school year, I think, *and included me in on your planning.* The thing that annoys me is that this is not the first time he has planned a vacation without my input. And I know it won't be the last. In my heart, I know if I speak my thoughts it will lead to an argument, one I'll be accused of starting. One I will surely lose. I let it go, and smile. "I can't wait. It'll be a lot of fun."

Twelve

W
e have returned home from our impromptu family getaway to Orlando. The week was long and adventurous. The boys enjoyed themselves. Surprisingly, I did as well. Twice, Randy allowed me to sleep in and lounge around the villa while he took the boys out. He even suggested I spend a day at the spa, pampering myself. This surprised me. But it's what I've needed—time for me. I longed to write in my journal, but was too afraid to bring it with me for fear that Randy would find it and read it. This morning, alarm clocks go off, footsteps are about the house, voices float throughout the rooms, reminding me that the vacation is over. After Randy is gone, the boys are off to school, and the triplets are settled, I retrieve my journal and begin my entry:

My mind is a collection of experiences, memories swirling. Words and actions have singed my soul. I am taunted and haunted by the unexpected. Everything I feel, everything I think, everything I see, everything I have become has been shaped by the hands of my husband. With every fiber of my being, I love him. But I don't like him. I admire him. But I fear him. I want him. But I no longer want to need him. Or depend on him. I want to find the woman lost in the wilderness of uncertainty. Want to recover the woman robbed of dreams, and visions, and hopes. I want this. Desire this. Yet, I want to believe my husband's words, his promises. I want to rise above this, want to move on from this. I don't want to keep wandering, searching, and hoping to find the missing pieces. Still, I hold my breath, wondering if I ever can. Wondering what will be waiting for me at the end of this journey.

❖❖❖

I am sitting in the waiting area of Dr. Curtis's office, flipping through the latest edition of *Jet*. The soft sounds of Lalah Hathaway gently float in the air. I listen intently. Try to recall the name of the CD. *Outrun the Sky. That's it*, I think, smiling. I glance at my timepiece. It's 1:15 p.m.

Dr. Curtis comes to the door, invites me in, then steps aside as I enter his space. I take my usual spot on his sofa, sink into its softness, then immediately apologize for canceling last week's appointment.

"You've never missed a session," he says with a smile. "I wasn't sure if I should be worried or not."

I appreciate his concern. "No, actually," I say, returning a smile. "Everything has been great."

"Why don't you tell me what's been going on."

I settle back, cross my legs, and share the events that have unfolded. How Randy whisked us off to Florida for a week. How the past two weeks have been the best in a long time. How he has spent time with the boys, and me. His attentiveness, his affection, seem surreal.

"He even says he's willing to go to marriage counseling," I say, looking directly at Dr. Curtis. "He says he'll do whatever it takes for us to save our marriage."

Dr. Curtis listens intently, nods, then rubs his chin. "Wow. Sounds like he has been just full of surprises," he says.

"To say the least," I respond, smiling.

"I'm glad to hear things have been going well with you and Randy. And that he's open to getting help. But your husband's behavior isn't a marital problem," he says, deflating my balloon of optimism. "It's *his* problem. It's something he needs to work on in a specialized program, one designed specifically for batterers *before* marriage counseling should be considered."

"I don't know if he'll agree to that," I state solemnly.

"The first step toward him taking any responsibility for his behaviors must begin, and end, with him." He pulls out a card, writes on the back of it, then hands it to me. "Here's the number to an Alternatives to Abuse Program in the area. Give him the number and let him make the call."

"And if he doesn't?" I ask, somehow already knowing.

"Then I'd say he's unfortunately not ready for change."

"And if he's not ready for change?"

Dr. Curtis clasps his hands. "I believe you already know the answer to that."

I nod, glancing at my timepiece. It is almost two o'clock.

"I want you to read something," Dr. Curtis says, getting up.

I watch him walk over to his desk and shuffle through a pile of papers stacked neatly on top. He returns and hands me a sheet of paper with a heading that reads: *Domestic Violence Statistical Summary.* It is part of a Uniform Crime Report prepared by the New Jersey State Police, highlighting the statistics for domestic violence in 2006. He has highlighted some of the text with a yellow marker. For some reason, my hand begins to shake as I hold the paper. I read: "There were 73,749 domestic violence offenses reported by the police in 2006." My heart skips when I see that there were forty-two murders as a result of domestic violence. Wives were the victims in twenty-one percent,

15,104, of the reported domestic violence offenses. Overall, females were victims in seventy-seven percent, 56,661, of all the offenses. *Oh my God*, I think. *How many more were there that weren't reported?* I hand the report back to him, stunned. My heart feels heavy as reality sets in. I am one of the many women who are in a violent relationship and haven't reported their abuse, for whatever reason. My chest tightens as I wonder how many victims, how many casualties, there were in 2007. Will these numbers be worse in 2008?

"Doctor Curtis, what causes people to do this...I mean...to be violent toward the ones they say they love?" I ask, reluctantly half-admitting my own situation, thankful it hasn't come to that extreme. Or has it?

"It is a learned behavior that is unfortunately reinforced by belief systems regarding gender roles and stereotypes," he explains. "Choosing to use violence in relationships to get what you want when you know there aren't going to be any negative consequences makes it much easier to be violent. Individuals who become violent or abusive in their relationships don't view their behavior toward their intimate partners as a crime. So the family is a safe place for violence to occur because there is a belief that what happens in the privacy of one's home, behind closed doors, is no one's business. Bottom line, violence, or threats of violence, are used to punish and to gain power over others, and to control them or the situations.

"Batterers *choose* to control their partners with rage, tantrums, taunts, threats, fists, force, and weapons. Through the use of intimidation, manipulation, and coercion they attempt to instill fear. Consequently, they emotionally scar, physically hurt, and, perhaps murder their significant others and children."

I don't know what I'd do if you ever tried to leave me. "It just sounds so...desperate," I say, pulling in a deep breath.

"In their minds, in their distorted thinking, it is. And sadly, over the years I've been in this field I've seen boyfriends turn into stalkers and husbands turn into killers. That's not to say that women aren't capable of being batterers as well, because they are. But statistics show that ninety to ninety-five percent of victims of domestic violence are women. And women who attempt to leave their abusers are at seventy-five percent greater risk of being killed than those who stay."

A chill runs through me. *I'm never letting you go.* "How many actually get away?" I ask, feeling the weight of what he just said fall on my chest. I try to steady my heartbeat.

"Not enough," he says, shaking his head. "The two most dangerous times for a woman are when she moves out and leaves her abuser, and when she tries to start a new relationship. The fear of being killed keeps many women in violent relationships. And, disturbingly, statistics back up this fear. Sadly, those who do attempt to leave will return to their abuser approximately eight or nine times before they are emotionally and mentally able to leave for good."

I shudder. Have a hard time trying to imagine someone being so vicious that they'd take the life of someone else in their dangerous attempt to keep them. *I think I'd lose my mind, and go crazy.* When the bell goes off signaling that my time is up, I get up. I leave my session with Dr. Curtis, feeling neither better nor worse.

Thirteen

It's four-thirty when I arrive home. K'wan and Kyle are in the great room doing homework. I give them kisses, then pay the sitter for watching the triplets and send her on her way. *I don't know why I can't keep them in day care*, I think, walking into the kitchen. Randy believes it's a waste of his money for them to be in day care all day, although he does allow me to send them half-days two days out of the week to allow me time to run my...I mean, his errands. Still, he thinks his children should be taught at home until kindergarten. I wonder what he'll do when they become of school age. *Want another baby*, I answer in my head.

I glance at my watch, and realize I have an hour or so before Randy gets home. I go upstairs, enter my walk-in closet, pull out my already packed suitcases, then check to make sure I haven't forgotten anything. I double-check to be sure I have my flight information. I sigh, wishing I did not have to resort to sneaking behind Randy's back. But he has left me no alternative. Not being at my mother's surprise party is not an option. *He's left me no other choice*, I think, removing my clothing, then going into the bathroom to take a quick shower. I stare at myself in the mirror, rub my stomach. "I'm sorry, but I will not have another baby," I say to myself, stepping into the steamy water.

Although I feel a twinge of guilt, I am glad I decided to visit my gynecologist a few weeks ago. Preventing Randy from keeping me barefoot and pregnant meant taking control of my body without conflict, which meant keeping my visit a secret. I couldn't chance getting caught with birth control pills, so out of all the available contraceptives I opted for an IUD. As embarrassing as it is for me to talk about, I shared my current marital situation with my GYN who agreed not to bill our insurance company. I was relieved. This visit, along with going to South Carolina against Randy's wishes, was the first real decision I have made for myself in years. It was my first step toward independence.

Bits and pieces of my session today with Dr. Curtis are still with me as I head downstairs to prepare dinner. "Batterers *choose* to control their partners... It is a learned behavior... Your husband's behavior isn't a marital problem. It's *his* problem."

For some reason, today I think about the constant scrutiny Randy has kept me under over the years, and how it affects me mentally. Every time I lift a fork to my mouth, he's watching me. Or telling me I'm overeating. Every time he thinks I've gained a pound, he's *advising* me about my weight. Every time I wear something that he believes is too revealing, he's accusing me of cheating. Every time I leave the house and stay longer than he thinks I should have, he's checking the mileage. I constantly feel like I'm under a microscope, being dissected into tiny pieces. And each time he cuts into me, opens me up, he leaves me feeling exposed and vulnerable. He says he does what he does out of care and concern for me. That he worries. That he loves me. At one time, I believed him. But now I think differently. *This is not about me. His behaviors are not about me.* I have to keep repeating this in my head. Have to commit this to memory. Have to keep telling myself this in order to maintain my own sanity.

Snatches of an argument with Randy a few years back resurface in my thoughts. He became agitated with me for not preparing a roast for Sunday dinner exactly the way his mother did. I had kept it in the oven thirty minutes longer than the recipe called for, and this displeased him. "Can't you do anything right?" he barked. "I specifically had my mother write out her recipe for you, and you still screw it up. Now the meat is overcooked and dry. I like my roast medium rare, not well done. You should know this by now!"

"It was an accident," I explained. "I got sidetracked with the baby. Kavon was crying and needed to be changed and fed."

He rolled his eyes. "Just once, I wish you'd do something right around here." He brushed past me, snatching a potholder from off the counter, then dumping the meat in the trash. "My parents will be here in another hour or so, so I suggest you figure out something else to cook. And don't mess it up."

I stood in the middle of the kitchen seething. I had been up early that morning cooking, baking, cleaning, and taking care of the babies. I had been on my feet practically all day, and I was exhausted. Before I realized it, I blurted out, "I'm leaving you. I can't take this anymore."

"Leaving to go where?" he snapped. "If you think I'll ever let you leave me, you are sadly mistaken. So stop talking stupid. You are my wife, 'til death do us part. And this is where you'll stay. Now find something else for us to eat before my parents get here." He headed for the doorway, then turned back around. "And another thing, just so I make myself very clear. Before I ever let you walk out of my life, I'll kill you first." His eyes never blinked. He walked out, leaving me slack-jawed. Those words have remained stuck in my head. *I'll kill you first.* I want to believe that they are just empty threats. But…how can I ever be sure?

I try to decide how I will broach the subject with Randy. How will I get him to agree to a domestic violence intervention group?

I hear the question in my head. *And if he doesn't?* The answer follows behind, loud and clear. *Then I'd say he's unfortunately not ready for change.* Randy has said he's willing to do whatever he needs to for us to get back on track. I have to believe he has said this because it is what he feels, what he wants, and needs. Not because it's what he believes I want to hear, but because it is his truth. It is his offering. His response tonight will decide what's real, and what's imagined.

❖❖❖

Dinner has been eaten, the kitchen cleaned, and the boys are preparing for bed. Randy is in his study when I finally decide to approach him.

"Offenders program?" He snorts indignantly. "This sounds like it's for some common criminal. I don't want to be around that type of element."

"It's not that kind of group," I offer, stealing glances around the room. "It's for domestic violence. It focuses on relationship issues, discusses the dynamics of abuse, and there are all types of men from different backgrounds…"

"You think I'm abusive?" he asks, narrowing his eyes.

Yes, I think. But, if I tell him the truth, it will most likely escalate into a fight. If I don't, then I remain stuck in denial. I give him a half-truth, stretched and twisted. "I believe you love me. But you are under a lot of stress that you sometimes take out on me. And you sometimes say and do things when you get angry that you really don't want to." I hear Doctor Curtis say *It's not about anger.*

"I thought you wanted *us* to go together. And now you're coming up with this group nonsense with a bunch of misfit men I have nothing in common with. Where's all this coming from?"

No, you *wanted us to go together.*

I think, consider. "Doctor Curtis thinks couples counseling is a great idea," I state gently. "But he believes it would benefit us both if we went to separate counseling first—only for a while."

"I don't need that kind of counseling," he states flatly. "I don't know what you're telling that doctor of yours, but I'm not the one with the problem."

His words sting, and I struggle hard not to crumble beneath their weight. In his eyes, everything is my fault, my problem. I wonder what happened to the man, who two weeks ago, was willing to do whatever it took. *This is not a marital problem...it is not your problem.* In his stare, I see his demanding need for affirmation. I look away. "I'm not saying that, Sweetheart," I say. "I just want you to please think about it...for us."

The muscles in his face twitch. He studies me for a moment. "I'll think about it," he finally says, glancing at the card one last time before folding it and tossing it up on his desk.

I force a smile, then walk over and plant a soft kiss on his lips. A kiss that holds very little meaning for me, but speaks volumes for him. It is a peace offering. An invitation for what's to come. He pats me on the rear.

"I'll be up in a minute," he replies, turning his attention back to his computer screen.

"Okay," I say, easing my way out the door, thankful this didn't turn into an argument, and he at least didn't say no.

❖❖❖

At this moment, there is a wind blowing, and I am being lifted, propelled in air, sweeping through space and time. Haphazardly, I am gliding and colliding. Fast and frantic, I am heading in a direction over which I have no control. I am being pulled and pushed by a force greater than me. No matter how hard I try to make sense out of this sojourn, there is something blocking my vision; something prevents me from seeing where the road ends and begins. And I am afraid of what awaits ahead.

"Thank you."

"I have one and she's a handful. I couldn't imagine having five. How do you do it?"

"With a lot of patience," I offer, smiling.

"I hear that. So, are you from Charlotte?" she asks as she punches in my information. Her long, manicured fingers rapidly hit the computer keys.

"No. I'm from here."

"Oh, okay. My sister just bought a townhouse in Charlotte and has been bugging me about moving down there. But I'd lose my mind that far from the city. I'm a Jersey girl."

"I feel the same way," I say.

"How many bags will you be checking?"

"Just these two," I say pointing to the two suitcases beside me. Another attendant reaches for them, places each one on the scale. They don't exceed the weight requirements. For once, besides the guilt I am carrying, I've packed light. He places them on the conveyor belt. "Okay. Here are your boarding passes," she says, handing me my tickets and returning my identification. "Gate Forty-five. Enjoy your flight."

"Thank you," I say.

"Mommy," K'wan says, giggling. "That lady thought me and Kyle were your brothers. We don't look *that* old."

"No," I correct him, grinning. "*I* don't look that old." He finds the notion humorous.

"Yes you do," he teases.

"Don't hate," I say, swatting him playfully. He ducks.

"Is Daddy coming, too?" Kyle asks, ignoring the banter between his brother and me.

"No," I reply. "Not this time."

Fourteen

S pring's morning sun is beaming, its rays warm and inviting. I wonder if it will be a hot summer as I pull my designer shades down over my eyes. Tomorrow is my mother's surprise party and the children and I are en route to North Carolina sans Randy. I arrive at the airport two hours early and I am glad it isn't as packed as I expected. When I reach the ticket counter, the young agent offers a friendly smile and says, "Identical triplets. They are so adorable."

I glance at her name tag. "Thank you, Juanita," I say proudly, handing her my e-ticket information and ID.

She looks at K'wan and Kyle. "Are those your brothers?"

They giggle. I smile, shaking my head. "No. They're mine as well."

"For real?" she asks with amazement. "Girl, they are gonna be fine when they get older." Both boys grin. "Oh my God, and they have the cutest dimples. Humph. You're gonna have to beat the girls off them."

"Juanita," I say jokingly, "let's hope I don't have to hurt 'em too bad."

"I know that's right," she says, chuckling and giving me the once-over, then studying my driver's license. "Five kids? Girl, you look good."

"Is he gonna be mad that we're going to see Grandma?" His question surprises me.

"Of course not," I fib. "Why would you ask that?"

He shrugs. But I know the answer. He's overheard more than he should.

"He never does anything with us," K'wan states matter-of-factly. I can hear the disappointment in his voice. Can feel it. And it cuts deep.

"That's because your father has to work," I explain. But they are both more perceptive than I like to acknowledge. I'm certain they know it's a lie—like most everything else in my life.

When we finally board, I strap the triplets in. K'wan and Kyle argue about who'll sit by the window. Kavon starts whining. He wants to sit on my lap.

"Not now," I say, rubbing his face. "Mommy will hold you when we get in the air." Of the three, he tends to be the most demanding of my time. When the plane finally ascends and it's safe to unfasten our seatbelts, I hold him in my arms and allow him to smother me with kisses. Eventually, he, along with his brothers, falls asleep. I close my eyes relieved to be able to nap as well.

After we land, I pull my carry-on from under the seat and wait for the plane to stop. I look over and the triplets are still sleeping. K'wan and Kyle are engrossed in their hand-held video games. I smile away my anxiety that surfaces as I think of how Randy will react when he gets home and finds us gone. I have left him a note, but know he'll be livid that I've defied him, gone against his wishes. I know I should have told him we were leaving today. Should have stood up to him. But I couldn't, didn't want to. Facing his wrath when I return is inevitable. I

am prepared to suffer the consequences. At least that is what I tell myself.

❖❖❖

The morning has been busy and the afternoon is no better. Janie's eight-bedroom, five-bathroom estate is full of people and noise—car doors slamming shut, the opening and closing of house doors and incessant ringing of the doorbell, footprints on freshly vacuumed carpets, echoes of laughter drifting from every room. Cars and SUVs fill the driveway and line the street next to her winding sidewalk. Relatives I haven't seen in years have driven and flown in to be a part of our mother's celebration. Most have checked into hotels; but have decided to gather at Janie's. Her home is where memories will be relived and new ones created.

Despite the recent miscarriage my niece has suffered and being released from the hospital only the night before, Janie—always the perfect hostess—flits around the house greeting everyone with a warm hug and inviting smile as if her life is in perfect order. As far as she's concerned, it is. She tells everyone Simone is on bed rest, battling a stomach virus. There will be no mention of her ever being pregnant. The entire incident will be brushed under the rug, and life will go on. And I understand.

The women, young and old, have taken up space in the large, gourmet kitchen. They will share tales, and laughter, and wisdom while preparing the family feast. The onslaught of fresh collards and string beans, candied yams, macaroni and cheese, potato salad, barbecue chicken, roast turkey, fried fish, beef ribs dripping with Aunt Edie's special sauce, along with

peach cobbler, bread pudding and homemade rolls makes mouths water and stomachs flip with anticipation. When everything is ready, the feast will be served on fine china and flatware. We will sit around an elegant marble table, under a Waterford chandelier, in Janie's massive dining room with its polished teak floor, and give thanks.

My cell phone begins to ring relentlessly around one o'clock. Each time, it has been Randy, irate. He's home and has found the note I've left. I try to calm him, let him know we'll only be gone a few days. It doesn't matter.

"I want you and *my* kids on the next plane back to Jersey. Do you understand me?" he snarls into the phone.

"Randy, that's not possible," I say defiantly. "My mother's surprise party is tomorrow."

"I don't give a damn. I told you not to go and I want you home. I've called the airline and there's a five-thirty flight. I expect you on it. Do you hear me?"

"Randy," I whisper, "I'm sorry if you're upset. But we'll be home on Sunday."

"I don't think you heard me!" he yells. "If you don't have your ass on that flight tonight, I will have you charged with kidnapping! Do you understand me? I did not give you permission to take my sons out of state. I want you home tonight." His threat paralyzes me for a moment.

I lower the volume on the phone, hoping no one else has heard him. Suddenly, I feel as if a spotlight has been placed on me, amplifying my every move. I catch Janie's stare and feel several pairs of eyes on me. I force a smile and walk into a room where there is no audience.

"Randy, please. It's only for a few days."

"I don't care. I want you on that plane. If not, all your shit will be out on the curb."

I no longer want to continue this one-sided discussion. The damage is already done. And I know I will pay dearly. "I love you too," I offer. "See you on Sunday." I hang up.

I take a deep breath, squeeze the tension from my eyes, and try to collect myself. When I turn to join the others, Janie is standing behind me. She startles me. "Is everything all right?" she asks, her eyes narrowed with suspicion.

"Of course," I reply, shifting my weight from one foot to the other. "Randy just forgot we were leaving today. That's all." I let out a nervous chuckle. "He's been so busy with work, it completely slipped his mind."

She raises her brow. "Hmmm." She eyes me cautiously, sensing my lie, but says nothing more. Under the blaze of her intense stare I feel my resolve slowly melting. I want to cry. I want to throw my arms around my sister and pour my heart out. But as much as I want to share, to lay down my burdens, I can't, and I won't.

"Let's get back to the others," I say, forcing a wide smile on my face. She walks over and gives me a hug, then kisses me on the cheek.

"I'm so glad you're here," she says.

I squeeze her tighter. "So am I."

❖❖❖

Dinner is over. The kitchen is clean and everyone is now stretched out throughout the house, watching movies, listening to music, and engaging in lively chitchat. I walk out onto the backyard deck where it is quiet. Above me, the moon is full and bright against a blackened sky sprinkled with twinkling stars. Closing my eyes, I inhale the peacefulness of the night. Despite its serenity I'm in turmoil. My mind starts to wander in no particular direction. Thoughts of a less-complicated life begin to find me. Life the way it once was splatters against a canvas of emptiness. I want my husband back. The man I laughed with. The man I felt safe with. The man I loved more than the air I breathe. I want once again the unbridled passion we once shared. I wonder what has gone wrong. Is it something I said or didn't say? Maybe forgot to say. Is it something I did, or didn't do, that has caused this shift in my marriage? I long for Randy's love. The gentle touch that once sent chills down my spine, made my soul erupt with desire. With all that is in me, I struggle to figure out what I have done wrong. My search comes up blank. There is nothing I can find.

The glass deck door opens. I hear shuffling behind me, but don't turn to see who it is. A few minutes later, Aunt Edie is standing beside me. She is my mother's oldest sister. At eighty-seven, she is the matriarch of the family.

"What's on your mind, child?" she asks.

I shake my head. "Nothing really," I say.

Her gray eyes narrow, adjusting in the darkness to see what I am concealing. "Now I might be old, but I ain't senile. I see more than I should, and I hear even more. So, you can try to hide it if you want, but I see it behind your eyes."

I smile, fighting back tears that gather in the wells of my eyes. "I'm fine, Aunt Edie, really."

"Baby," she says, her face softening as she pats my hand. This is how she will begin, sharing, giving her wisdom. "I was young once. I've had my share of heartaches and disappointments. I married your Uncle Bert, God rest his soul, when I was sixteen years old. I stayed married to him for sixty-eight years before the good Lord took him from this earth three years ago, and believe me, he was no saint. That man was as ornery as a bull in heat. But I loved him right up till the night he died. And don't you think for one moment that loving and staying didn't come with many sacrifices and tears shed. Not that I regret my choices. But if I had it to do all over again, I'd have done it much different."

I look at her, surprised at what she's saying. Is she telling me what I think she is? I wonder. "How so?" I ask. "You and Uncle Bert seemed so happy together."

"For the most part," she says, "we were. But what we sometimes think we see on the outside isn't always what is. I know he loved me in the best way he knew how. He just didn't always know how to show it in the right way. Anyway, I would have loved me more," she states, looking off, drifting down memory lane, a crossing I allow her to take alone.

The moon's illumination falls on her face. She stands with a quiet elegance I admire. She's wearing a long, navy-blue linen dress and navy-blue shoes. A strand of pearls drapes her narrow neck. With her shiny silver hair pinned back in a bun, I catch the glint of a diamond in her right ear. She looks much younger than her age. Her pecan-colored skin is smooth. *Good black don't crack*, I hear. It's something she has said many times over the years. I smile to myself.

"In my time," she continues, returning her attention to me, "you made sacrifices that included giving up many parts of yourself. You learned to turn the other cheek and make do with what you had. A woman stayed in her place. Cooking and cleaning and tending to her family, and minding her manners, that's what a woman was supposed to do. It is what she was expected to do. She had no voice. Your husband was the head of the household, and you didn't question him. You didn't go against him. You held your tongue and stood by him, no matter what.

"But, I'm telling you, if I could turn back the hands of time, I would have gotten my education, traveled and experienced the world a bit, and not had so many babies, not all at once, anyway." She chuckles. "Not that I don't love my children. I'm proud of them. Watching them grow is what filled me with joy. They were my life. And they've done very well for themselves, all twelve of 'em. " She leans in and lowers her voice. "But each time I got pregnant, I felt like I'd given up a piece of myself I'd never get back. By the time they were all grown up and on their own, so much time had gone by that I felt like there was no sense chasing dreams, looking for the missing parts of my life. So I stayed and made do with what I had. That was my choice. To love the best way I knew how. To forgive, and learn to accept the things I would never be able to change.

"I had to let go of all the what-ifs I held on to, and embrace life for what it was. A journey. My journey. No matter where I ended up, it was my choices that brought me there. So, baby," she says, stroking my hair, "find your voice and stop holding on to things that keep you weighed down. Love is what love does. Always remember that." Her hand rests on my back. She rubs it. "The one thing I've learned in life is: Fear is what will either keep you running, or holding on. It is what will keep you a victim of circumstance. If you live in yesterday, if you abandon today, you will never get to where you want to be tomorrow. Every day is a choice."

Every day is a choice. For a moment, I think Dr. Curtis is

speaking to me through her. I shake the notion from my head.
I wonder if Aunt Edie knows just how wounded I am. It is at this
moment I believe she can see the scars that I keep out of sight.
Buried beneath smiles. Obscured by the trappings of the life
Randy has provided for me. I glance down at my huge diamond
ring. Its sparkle dances under the light, betraying the darkness
in my heart. A sob finds its way to the back of my throat. I
swallow it. Allow it to settle in the pit of my soul, hidden. I
hug her tight. No other words are spoken. None are needed.
I have found comfort in everything she has said. The message
is clear: My starting point must be today. I can't explain it but
something loosens inside of me and I feel liberated, at least
temporarily. I embrace this newness, no matter how brief,
kissing the fleshy softness of Aunt Edie's cheek before walking
back inside to bask in the comforts of family.

Fifteen

It is ten p.m. Randy's voice takes me by surprise. He is standing in the middle of the kitchen, hugging and kissing everyone. Our eyes meet. He glances at me, smirking, every few seconds over the shoulders of the crowd that swarms around him. My freedom has come and gone. He senses this and smiles widely, breaking away from his admirers. Triumph in his swagger, he walks over to me. "Hey, baby," he says, planting a kiss on my lips. He takes my hand, squeezes, kisses me again, then wraps his arm around my waist, pulling me into him. "I was able to catch a later flight, and thought I'd come down to join the festivities. I know how much you wanted me to be here." I force a smile. His words and gestures, light and loving, drip with a hidden threat. Yet, he plays the role of adoring husband. His script is neatly prepared. He knows how to say the right things at the right times. The room glows. Everyone is happy to see him. He charms them. Convinces them how wonderful he is. No one will ever believe that underneath his captivating persona, there's a dark, ugly side that he will share, behind the comforts of closed doors, only with me. Aunt Edie's eyes become flares of concern. I avoid her gaze. Afraid it will expose too much.

❖❖❖

It is a little after one in the morning. The house has finally settled. We are in the guestroom down the hall from Janie and Rodney, and the boys are all sharing a room across from Randy and me. Randy's pasted smile has been replaced with a scowl, but he says nothing. He undresses. I go into the bathroom and turn on the shower. When the bathroom steams, I close the door, remove my clothes, and step in. I need to wash away the tension that coils itself throughout my body, wrapping around my spirit, slowly strangling me. After the way he spoke to me earlier on the phone, his unexpected presence is not what I had hoped for, or needed. I replay bits of Aunt Edie's conversation in my head. "Find your voice... Fear is what will either keep you running, or holding on. It is what will keep you a victim of circumstance." My mind is like a recorder. I press rewind and recall my last visit with Dr. Curtis. "Statistics state women who attempt to leave are at seventy-five percent greater risk of being killed than those who stay." *But I don't want to leave*, I think. *I just want things to get better.* Still, the thought causes my stomach to quiver, and triggers a wave of nausea that is difficult for me to shake.

I lather up and begin scrubbing my face and body. I am so consumed in my thoughts of what my life has become that I don't hear Randy enter the bathroom. He steps into the shower, robbing me of my space.

"You enjoy making me angry," he whispers in my ear, pressing himself against me. "Don't you?"

He startles me. I try to remove soap and water from my eyes. Try to rinse away the sting. "No," I say. "That isn't my intention."

"Don't lie to me," he says. His eyes are tight, full of madness. "The deal was I get a threesome, and you get to visit your family." The muscles in his jaws tighten. "You refused. But you came down here anyway. I don't know why you insist on disrespecting me."

He snatches the washrag out of my hand, swats me in the face with it, then pins me up against the wall with my arms up over my head. "Just wait until I get you home." His voice is harsh and raspy in my ear. "I haven't put my hands on you in a while, so when I do, you'll know why."

I want to yell for help. However, the thought of my abuse being exposed to my sister and her family keeps my scream lodged in the back of my throat. Somehow, I know he won't hurt or injure me now, not here.

"Do it now, Randy," I say, trying to conceal my fright. "Just beat me now and get it over with."

Randy knows me well enough to know that my words carry no real meaning. That what I have said is as empty as the look in his eyes. "Don't tempt me," he replies, squeezing my wrists.

"Oww," I say. "You're hurting me."

He ignores me. Squeezes me tighter. Grinds into me, then bites down on my bottom lip hard enough to make me wince without drawing blood. His manhood stiffens against me. His adrenaline surges, like a violent wave. He pries my legs open, then shoves himself in me. "You belong to me. I am never letting you go. And you will learn to do what I say, when I say it." His thrusts are erratic, rapid and deep, piercing me. There is no passion in his movements. His grunts are hauntingly familiar, but emotionally disconnected. I blink and stare at the wall in distressed silence. I am being raped by my husband. A tear escapes from my eye and slides down my already wet face. In my heart, I know this is just the beginning of what lies ahead. But I will get through tonight. Endure the pain. Keep quiet. And tomorrow I will celebrate my mother's birthday, hide behind my mask, and face my family with a smile.

❖❖❖

We are now on our way back home. When the plane hits cruising altitude, I close my eyes and flip through snapshots of the weekend. My mother's party was beautiful, and she was truly surprised. It felt good to be around family. I've felt so isolated, which only increases my insecurity. My mother's face darts across my thoughts. Her eyes lit up like a Christmas tree the moment she opened Randy's gift—a two-carat, diamond-encrusted cross on a platinum chain. I wonder how he found time to purchase the extravagant gift. He hangs it around her neck, then smothers her with kisses. He is the son she's always wanted. She beams, snatching glances at me. That she will wear her necklace proudly sickens me. That she will continue to remind me of how wonderful he is makes my heart fill with dread.

Sitting here now, next to Randy, I steal a sideways glance at him. He has said nothing the whole flight. He sits next to me, rigid and cold. How he managed to return on the same flight baffles me. But I know better than to ask, so I try to let it go. Try not to let it rent space in my head. Sadly, it does.

Once we arrive at Newark International Airport, we make our way through the mass of people to the baggage claim, then to the airport shuttle. When we finally reach my truck, Randy and the boys load the back with our luggage. I fasten the triplets into their seats, then slide into the passenger side. My stomach is turning and twisting into knots of stress. I think back on the last two weeks, and how loving and attentive Randy had been. I hear Dr. Curtis in my head. His voice is crisp and clear. "It's the honeymoon stage. It's only a matter of time before he explodes again."

Randy gets in, then backs out of our space. He pays the parking fee, and exits toward the turnpike for the twenty-five-minute drive to our upscale community in Alpine, New Jersey.

In no time, the boys fall asleep. The entire ride home is deadly silent. I recline my seat and close my eyes, pretend to be asleep. I feel Randy's eyes on me, and I know he knows, senses, it's all an act.

As soon as we enter the house, a frightening stillness hovers over me like a dark-bellied cloud, waiting to explode. I feed the kids, give them their baths, put them to bed, hoping my tasks will give Randy enough time to unwind, hoping he will let go of his anger at my decision to spend time with my family. Unfortunately, he doesn't. He watches me through slits of quiet rage.

When we are on the other side of our bedroom door, when Randy thinks the boys are sound asleep down the hall and it is safe, he walks calmly across the room, backs me up against the wall, and slaps me so hard my ears ring. The room begins to shake and spin and I see stars. My lips tremble. I feel dizzy. But I stand planted in place. The fire in his eyes burns through me. It is the calm before the storm. His face darkens. The muscles in his jaws tighten. I brace myself. Harsh words will come like an angry, thrashing wind.

I try not to look into the eyes of my husband for fear I'd see no trace of the man I fell in love with. I step to the side, attempt to find shelter from what's to come. He blocks me. I step to the other side, and he blocks me again.

"Don't. You. Ever. Fucking embarrass me, or disregard what I tell you, again! You don't take *my* sons anywhere without discussing it with me first."

"Randy, I did discuss it with you," I offer, holding the side of my face.

"And I didn't give you my permission," he snaps. "I told you I didn't want you taking them, and you said you wouldn't. But you go behind my back and take them anyway. You lied to me."

I don't recall this conversation, me saying I wouldn't take them; can't remember ever lying to him. But he tries to convince me otherwise. "Randy—"

"Just shut your trap before I put my fist in it. I don't wanna hear none of your crap. You're nothing but a fucking liar. I'm sick of you constantly trying to undermine my authority. What do I have to do to get you to do what I tell you, break your damn jaw or something, is that it?" His verbal lashing cracks like a whip across my back. Stings. Burns. Exposes my flesh. He intends to leave scars. His nostrils are flaring. I shrink back. Try to put some distance between us.

"Randy, please. You'll wake the kids." I say this, hoping it will make a difference. It doesn't.

"Don't you try to pull the kids into this," he hisses. "You started this with your lies and sneakiness. So you have no one to blame but yourself."

"Randy, I don't want to fight with you," I say, trying to get past him. He grabs me. I twist away from him. Try to escape. But he yanks me by the hair and throws me to the floor.

"Don't you fucking walk away from me when I'm talking to you," he snaps. "I'll break your damn face!" His loafer-clad foot connects with the side of my face. I roll. Hold my head. Try to block his blows. Dodge his raised foot. "I will kick your fucking teeth down your throat."

Instinctively, I curl myself into a ball. He kicks and stomps me. Somehow he is now on top of me, pounding me with his fists, the blows getting heavier as his words become sharper. "I'm fucking sick of you disrespecting me in my own house. I pay the fucking bills here. And you'll do what I say or I will fucking kill you." A thick explosion of pain bursts through me. Yet, I keep my screams bottled in the back of my throat. For the sake of my children, I become mute. My silence sends him over the edge. He places his hands around my neck, squeezes, and I am gasping for air. Kicking. Digging my nails into his hands. Trying to scratch my way free. This is not how I want my children to see or remember me—lifeless, strangled at the hands of their father.

My attempt to break free only adds fuel to his fire. "Oh you wanna fight, huh?" He punches me. "I'll give you something to fight." Punches me again. I stop. Surrender. Lie still. Give him what he wants. Control.

"Please," I plead. Beg.

"Why can't *you* just do what I ask, huh? Why do *you* make me have to act ugly to get you to fucking listen, huh? You must like your ass beat. Don't you?"

I no longer hear what he says. Instead, Dr. Curtis's voice begins to take up space in my mind, his words twirling, looping together. *You have to protect yourself. …Domestic violence hurts children, and families. …Whether you choose to stay or leave, the choice is yours. …He is responsible for his behavior, not you. …As long as you keep quiet, don't hold him accountable, he will continue to abuse you. ...His intent may not be to kill you, but it's definitely to instill fear in you. When that no longer works, the abuse will increase in severity.*

I try to concentrate, but everything is in a haze. Muffled. I am surrounded by a fog I can no longer bear. My mind drowns as sorrow swims behind my eyes. I blink, blink again. Lift the veil of pretense. Try to see what I've been afraid to see. Attempt to consider my options. I can continue to close my eyes to the truth. Continue to make excuses. Keep pretending. Remain quiet and compliant. Or take a stand. Intellectually, I know what I must do. Emotionally, I know whatever I decide, my life will be very different tomorrow.

My eyes plead with him.

A glimmer of sorrow, I think, comes across his face. He lets go.

Air quickly fills my lungs, burns me to the core. I cough up blood.

Gradually, he comes into focus. My eyes adjust and I begin to see the beast that has attacked me. I stare at him, then past him as he walks off to the bathroom, leaving me lying on the floor, dying inside. He shuts the door. The shower turns on. He will try to rinse off what he has done, then attempt—with no regret, no remorse—to console me and pretend that he has done nothing. I struggle to get up but can't. I am frozen. As hurtful as it is, I know, I acknowledge, that after almost twelve years of marriage, I am sleeping with the enemy. My life is in danger. His intention may *not* be to kill me, but his threats are real. They echo in my head. Become slingshots of reality. *"I will fucking kill you!"*

Discomfort and disbelief fill me. But I don't feel. I refuse to shed a tear. I am numb. I refuse to have my spirit smashed into any more pieces.

He has abused me.

He has bruised me.

He has confused me.

He has hurt me one time too many.

And I have cried my last tear.

My mind is made up. Tonight, the silence will be broken. I will not allow him to kill me. I will not continue to be his victim. It is a role that has taken too much out of me. I cannot bear the thought of police coming to our home, or my sons seeing their father being taken out in handcuffs, but remaining private, keeping our business behind closed doors is no longer a priority. Out of necessity, if I am to survive, he has to be held accountable.

Battered and in pain, I find the will to crawl toward the door. I pull myself up. I sneak out of our bedroom, limp downstairs and, with trembling fingers, dial 9-1-1. Slowly, as I shake, my voice comes in a strained whisper. "Help me," I say into the phone. "My husband has beaten me."

Sixteen

I n a flash, everything becomes a blur. My life has been
turned upside down. There is a no-contact order in place
until our court hearing. This is not what I want. I just want
the police to scare Randy, to get him to stop hitting me, not
arrest him. Not charge him with assault, harassment, and
terroristic threats. Not ban him from our home. Not set a five-
thousand-dollar bail. Just stop him from beating me. But the
police officer says if I don't cooperate, they'll be forced to call
DYFS on me. He says my children will be taken away from me.
My children are my life. I can never allow that to happen. So
I agree. When the officer asks if this is the first incident of
domestic violence, I lie and tell him yes. Something stops me
from revealing too much. I still feel the need to protect Randy.
Despite everything, he is *still* my husband. The officer looks at
me with disbelieving eyes. He doesn't speak it, but it shows on
his face. He has seen and heard this many times before. I avert
my eyes. He offers to take me to the hospital. I refuse. They want
to take pictures. Again, I refuse.

Everything has happened so fast. My head is spinning. My face
and body are covered with black-and-blue bruises. And aches.
My muscles are tender and sore. I touch the side of my face

and feel the fresh sting of Randy's handprint. *This is the worst he's ever done,* I think, shuddering. As I watch them handcuff my husband, place him inside the patrol car, then pull off, I am wrestling with that part of me that wants to deny this is happening to me. That this is what has become of my life. Still, no matter how many times my head tells me what Randy is doing is wrong, that he has to be held accountable, that I deserve better, my heart still says he loves me—no matter what.

❖❖❖

I glance at the digital clock on my nightstand. It reads 7:00 a.m. The kids will stay home from school. I do not have the strength or energy to get out of bed to get them ready. Not today. I just want to curl up in a ball and lose myself. Become invisible. But I know I can't. My children depend on me. There is a light knock on my door. I rub my eyes, then run my hands through my hair. "Come in," I say, sitting up.

Kyle walks in. Behind him is K'wan carrying a tray. They are both in their pajamas. "I made you breakfast, Mommy," Kyle says, smiling.

I prop two pillows in back of me. "Thank you," I say, parting my lips in a slight smile. It hurts.

K'wan sucks his teeth. "You're such a liar," he snaps, brushing past his brother. "*We* made you breakfast." He hands me the tray. There is a plate of three Aunt Jemima blueberry waffles, Dole sliced tropical fruit, and orange juice. I appreciate the gesture. I know they know; know they saw and heard the events from the night before.

"Thank you," I say. Then I close my eyes and say grace. I take a slow sip of the juice. I am really not hungry, but don't want to offend them. "Where are your brothers?" I ask, placing my glass back on the tray.

"Still sleep," Kyle answers. He is standing at the foot of the bed. His eyes are glued to my face and neck. I place my hand up to my throat. Try to cover up their father's marks. K'wan sits beside me on the edge of the bed and holds his head down. Waves of embarrassment, guilt, despair, and shame wash over me.

I put a spoonful of fruit into my mouth, chew slowly, then force it down along with my scattered emotions.

"We saw the police take Daddy last night," Kyle says. "Did he hurt you?"

I swallow hard. I don't know how to answer him. I want to tell him yes. Tell him how much pain I am in, emotionally and physically. But I don't. "It's not as bad as it looks," I say, looking away. I take another slow sip of my juice.

"I hate him," K'wan blurts out, opening and closing his fists.

"Who?" I ask, already knowing.

"Daddy," he says. His nose flares.

"Don't talk like that," I say, setting my glass down and placing the tray to the side. I reach over and rub his back. "He is still your father."

"I don't care. I still hate him," he snaps, sounding much older than his age. "And I hope he never comes back."

"Look at me," I say softly. He turns his head toward me. Behind his wet eyes, I see a slow, burning fire. I rub the side of his innocent face. *Domestic violence affects children as well.* My heart trembles. "That's not a nice thing to say. No matter what your father and I are going through, he loves you."

Kyle is now kneeling, leaning on the bed. His chin rests on

his folded arms. "Does Daddy love you?" he inquires. His eyes narrow and become slits of uncertainty.

"Sure he does," I say.

His eyebrows crease. He stares down at the comforter and starts toying with its edges, picking at some imaginary lint.

Silence chokes the room. I take slow, deep breaths, searching for the truth. But it is hidden inside pockets of thick air.

"Your father loves me very much," I say, offering a flicker of hope. I try to give them something I think they will believe. The looks on their faces tell me they won't.

"Then why does he hit you?" K'wan asks in a voice that slices through me, cutting to the core of my soul.

My eyes avert his. "Because…" I look around the room, search for words I cannot find. His question requires an answer that feels too complicated to try to explain. They are both staring at me, waiting for a response. One I can't give. My eyes glisten. But I keep my tears at bay. I hold them back, pinch the bridge of my nose, then get out of bed.

K'wan and Kyle are watching me, counting my steps as I walk into my bathroom, and shut the door. Even behind the door, I still feel their intense gazes burning through me. I lock myself away from their curious, hurt eyes, then slide my back against the door, sitting down on the marble floor, listening to them on the other side.

"Is Mommy going to be okay?" Kyle whispers.

"Yes," K'wan says, "she'll be okay. I'm going to keep her safe."

"Me too."

I press my ear to the door and eavesdrop on my ten- and eight-year-olds talking about protecting me. Talking about not letting their father do anything else to hurt me. They feel it's their duty to keep me safe when it should be the other way around. *This is too much to bear*, I think, pulling my knees up to my chest and wrapping my arms tightly around them. Everything in me begins to shake. My lips quiver. My chest heaves in and out. I begin trembling and convulsing, rocking and swaying. With each jerk of my body, all the feelings—the loneliness, hurt, guilt, shame, and confusion—that have kept me chained to my fear swell and swirl, crashing against my heart. I close my eyes, lower my head, then allow an avalanche of hot, heavy tears to roll down my face and splatter onto the floor.

Seventeen

I t is one p.m. and raining hard. I do not want to leave the coziness of my bed. The triplets are lying in the space that belongs to Randy; Kyle and K'wan are in my sitting room watching *Tomb Raider*. Today they insist on staying close by. This comforts and saddens me. I don't want to sit or lie around feeling sorry for myself. My falling into a depression isn't good for them, or me. I decide that after my bath, I will order pizza and some Chinese food, watch movies, and enjoy their company. Try to ignore the emptiness that echoes in my heart.

I head for my bathroom, turn on the water, then pour in some jasmine and lavender bath crystals in the bottom of the tub. I disrobe, and avoid my reflection in the mirror. Refuse to see my shattered soul exposed. I step into the tub, and allow the bubbles and steam to take me away. I feel so weak, emotionally and mentally. I lay my head back, and think about Randy. The thought of our lives traveling different paths hurts like hell. It's a piercing, nerve-rattling pain that shoots through me, and causes tears to well up in my eyes. I close them, and rewind the hands of time until I can see the past. A time filled with promise, and hope, expectation, and bliss. Memories of my wedding day; the birth of each of my sons; the overwhelming joy that filled me each time Randy touched me, made love to me. I inhale deeply until I can smell his scent. Until I can feel the heat from his hands, taste the softness of his lips. Randy, Randy, Randy. *How could he do this to me?*

My mind fast-forwards, skips, to the present. To the forceful sex acts, and degrading requests. To the name-calling, and threats; to the slaps and punches; to the hurt and disappointment. Recollections of the phone being yanked from the wall, and me being locked out of the house come into view. I am barefoot and in my nightgown, banging on the door. Begging. Pleading. The kids are screaming and yelling. I am screaming and yelling. Randy is screaming and yelling. K'wan and Kyle come running from around the back of the house, clinging to me. They have escaped to come rescue me. They are crying. I am crying. I can hear the triplets crying. Finally the door opens, and I am let back in.

The tape in my mind continues to play. Things I have tried to block out come rushing back in crisp, vivid focus. K'wan is a baby. Randy and I are in our bedroom arguing. I run out of the room in tears, and I am almost at the stairs when he runs behind me, yanks me by the arm and swings me around. I snatch my arm back and... somehow I am slumped over. I see Randy's hand, see his knee midair but can't be certain if he slapped me, or kneed me. I can't be sure if I pulled something inside of me. The only thing I am certain of is that I am four months' pregnant, cramping and bleeding. My screams pierce through the house and Randy is in a panic as he calls 911 for help. I hear my infant son crying in the background. See my husband on his knees crying, begging for *me* to not lose our baby. His pleas go unheard. His tears go unchecked. Our unborn child's life flows out of me. By some unforgivable means this loss becomes my doing.

I blink, blink again. Try to shake the unpleasant memories from my mind. But they stick and remind me that I am battered and alone. I have suffered two miscarriages. I am on my own in sorting through this emptiness. This realization causes a knot to build in my throat. I am choking. Fighting for air; fighting for strength; fighting for courage. Fighting, fighting, fighting— to survive.

The unexpected ringing of the telephone snaps me out of my trance. At first I start not to answer, but I pick up on the fifth ring.

"Hello."

Silence.

"Hello," I say again. I know there's someone on the other end. I can hear slow, steady breathing. My hands shake.

"Is this what you really want?" he finally says. He sounds wounded, like someone has stabbed him a thousand times.

"No, Randy," I say. "But—"

"Then why did you call the police on me and have me locked up?" he asks, cutting me off.

I frown. He insists on blaming me. Not this time. "I didn't have you locked up, Randy. You did."

"But you called the police."

"And you beat me," I point out.

"I didn't mean to lose it like that," he replies. He says this as if everything else he has ever done or said to me is okay. As if he's only gone too far this time.

"You didn't lose anything, Randy. You knew way before we stepped foot in this house what you were going to do to me. It was planned. You know it, and I know it. So don't go there."

"Well...if you didn't go behind my—"

I don't allow him space to make excuses. There is no justification for his abuse. And I do not want to hear his list of reasons. "Bullshit, Randy!" I snap through clenched teeth. "This is not about me." The intensity of my voice surprises me. In all the years we've been together, I have never raised my voice, never cursed at him. "So don't you dare blame *me* for this predicament *you* put us in. I didn't ask for this. I didn't ask to get beat on. I didn't ask to be called bitches, and fat, lazy asses. I didn't ask to be told I would never be anything without you. That the only thing I was good for was having babies. I didn't ask to be threatened with having my kids taken from me, or being thrown out on the streets. *You* did this. Not me."

"I said all those things in anger. I didn't mean any of it," he insists. But I don't believe those words.

"But you said them. And you've hurt me more than once with your fists, and your words. I can't...I won't...live like that."

"I love you so much," he says, sniffling. His voice is wet with tears. "Don't you love me?" The question sounds frantic.

Yes, I love you, I think, but refuse to say. "Whether I love you or not is not the point, or the issue. I've stood by you, Randy. Put my life on hold for you. Abandoned anything I've ever wanted to do or be for your sake. I've been a wife and a mother. Been everything *you've* wanted and needed. And at the end of the day, I still have nothing for myself."

"Don't say that, baby. Please. You have me."

He and my emotions are getting the best of me. I wipe tears from my eyes. "No, Randy, I don't. I lost you a long time ago. And I've lost myself, waiting and hoping that you—the man I married, and loved, and gave every bit of myself to—would find your way back. I can't keep holding on."

His voice cracks, rises above a whisper. "Don't say that. Let me come home. I can't lose you. We can work this out. I can change. I will change. Baby, I just need you to believe in me. Not give up on me—on us. I'm begging you. I love you, sweetheart."

He is tugging at my heart, pulling my feelings apart. I remain mute, allowing him to continue. "Please, baby, don't do this to us. I am so sorry. Don't keep me from my family. I'll get help. You hear me? I promise. I'll do whatever it takes. I need you, baby. You and the boys are my life. Everything I am is because of you, and my sons."

I don't know if I believe what he says. But something scratching at the surface of my heart says try. Something says even if things don't work out, you have to at least give him a chance if not for the children, for yourself. I hear this loud and clear, ringing like church bells. Still, I'm afraid to permit what's inside of me to lead my thoughts or feelings. I don't want to hear the regret, remorse, or promises. I am overwhelmed by his wants and his needs. *What does Syreeta want?* Time, space, to find me, I answer in my head.

"I can't talk right now, Randy. I need time to think…to sort through my feelings," I say hurriedly, then hang up before I allow him to manipulate my emotions.

My water has turned cold, and my stomach is knotted with trepidation. I hurriedly dry myself off, then walk into my bedroom. The triplets are sprawled out on my bed, sleeping. K'wan and Kyle are downstairs. No matter how short, I welcome the quiet and enter my walk-in to retrieve my journal from its hiding place. I write:

Last Night I Cried

As I sat in complete silence
Listening to my thoughts
A collage of images
Began to swirl through my mind
Bursting with vibrant colors
Faces of beautiful women
Emerged
Converged
Blurred
Then disappeared

As I blinked my eyes
I slowly realized
They were the survivors of domestic violence

Suddenly
My chest tightened
And without warning
No matter how hard I fought
The tears began to fall
With an urgency
I never knew before
And I cried
For them all

I cried
Because my mother had cried
And my sisters had cried
And my aunts had cried
And my cousins had cried

I cried
Because my friends had cried

And women I never knew had cried
Strangers in my mind
I cried for the emotional turmoil
That depleted their spirit
And left them feeling empty
That kept them isolated

I fell down on my knees
And cried
With all my heart
And soul
For the undeserving heartache
The black eyes
Busted lips
Broken ribs
And nasty words
They had to endure

And as the tears rolled down my face
I thanked God
For giving them the courage
And the strength
And the conviction
To emotionally
Mentally
Physically
Spiritually
Find a way
To be free

And then
Last night
I cried

And prayed
For the ones who stayed
And weren't able to break away
Hoping
Believing
Things would change
If their lives could only be rearranged
Perhaps the future would be brighter
Maybe their burdens a little lighter
Sadly
Yesterday is haunting
Today remains a blur
Tomorrow will never come
Because they had died
And I cried
And cried
And cried
Clinging to pain
They didn't deserve
Holding on to broken promises
That they now take to their graves

Eighteen

The caller ID displays my mother's number. I take a deep breath, then pick up.

"Hello, Mother."

"Syreeta, what in heaven's name is going on up there?" my mother asks, firing a series of questions. "What is this mess about Randall being put out of his own home? Have you gone batty or what? I've been calling you all day."

"No, Mother," I say wearily. "But I really don't want to get into it. Not now."

"Well, I'm catching the next flight out. I need to understand what's going on."

"There's no need for that, Mother. Obviously, you've already spoken to Randy so you already know what's going on."

"I know Randall is distraught," she shares.

"Well, he should be," I reply. "Your beloved Randall beat me, and I called the police on him."

"And why in God's name would you do something like that?"

I feel a headache pushing its way to the front of my head. I squeeze my eyes shut, trying to will it away.

"Because he put his hands on me, and called me out of my name more than I can stand," I inform her. "And I'm not going to put up with it any longer."

"Don't you realize how much that man adores you?" she asks, dismissing what I have said. "He's given you the world."

"He's given me everything but respect," I say. "So if beating on me is how he shows his adoration for me, then I'd rather do without it."

"Well, what did you do to upset him this time?"

Again, as always, it is my fault. "I came to your party," I say harshly. "Without his permission."

"That's nonsense," she huffs. "You must have said or done *something* else. You had to have given him a reason to hit you. If you don't stop this ridiculous behavior, you'll end up by yourself."

My body stiffens. For several moments, I am locked in an unsettling silence. I try to steady my breathing, try to calm my nerves. I attempt to speak, but my tongue sticks to the roof of my mouth, preventing me from saying something I'll regret. All my life I have sought my mother's approval. Wanted her affection. Hoped for her support. Wished she'd embrace me with words of comfort, understanding. But no matter how long I wait, I am painfully aware that that day will never come. She will always make me feel incapable.

Her voice slices through my thoughts. "I don't know who is encouraging you to turn your back on your husband. But it needs to stop. I don't want you seeing that troublemaking doctor of yours anymore. He's filling your head with all sorts of nonsense. I don't know what kind of hold that doctor has on you, but if you don't end those sessions, it's going to cost you everything. You keep listening to him and you'll end up losing a good man."

Tears pour from my eyes. "Mother, will you stop? Just stop it! There's nothing good about any man who beats on his wife—

nothing. How dare you try to blame me for Randy's behavior," I hiss. Before I can stop myself, the floodgates open and everything I've ever wanted to say gushes out of me like a roaring ocean. "Or blame Doctor Curtis for helping me to finally stand up for myself. I've done nothing. I've been a good wife and mother. I've done nothing but love him and cater to Randy's every need and I'm tired of being his doormat and damn punching bag. All my life I've tried to be the daughter you wanted, but nothing I've ever done has been good enough for you. And I'm sick and tired of trying to live up to your expectations."

"Syreeta! You will not use that tone with me," my mother snaps. "Do you understand?"

I ignore her. Today, I am prepared for battle. "Well, stay out of my business," I retort. "If you can't offer anything constructive, I would rather you just keep quiet. I don't recall ever getting in the middle of your and Daddy's marriage. Not once did you stand up to him. Not once did I ever hear you say no to him. Everything was always 'Yes, dear,' this, 'Yes, dear,' that. I remember you being sick with the flu, and Daddy called out for you to make his breakfast because he was hungry. Instead of staying in bed and taking care of yourself, you practically crawled out of bed to slave over a hot stove to make him his breakfast. Then he fussed with you about making eggs and bacon because this particular day, he wanted pancakes and hash browns. How were you supposed to know that? You apologized to him for not asking, like it was your fault. And instead of you telling him you didn't feel well, you took his plate and staggered back over to the stove to make his pancakes. He stared at your back but never asked you if you were okay, never said, 'Sweetheart, go back to bed,' just watched you cough and shiver. I sat at the bottom of the stairs and watched all of this. And not once did you open your mouth. You had no backbone. You let him walk all over you. Why, Mother?"

"He was your father, but he was *my* husband. I loved him, and catering to him is what I chose to do because he was the father of my daughters, a hard-working man and a darn good provider. That man loved the ground I walked on, and only required that I raise our children, keep up with the house, have a home-cooked meal on the table, and take care of his needs. I did what I did because he was the man of the house. And if I had to do it all over again, I would. So don't you dare question me or my marriage to your father."

"Then why do you feel it's your duty to meddle in mine? I'm your daughter. You should be concerned about how I'm doing instead of worrying about *my* husband. I told you he beats me and has broken my spirit and the only thing you can ask is, 'What did you do to upset him,' as if I'm the cause of his abuse.

"I'm so sick of you always taking Randy's side as if he's above reproach. Well, newsflash, Mother: He's not the man you think he is. There's another side to him that is cruel and ugly. I have lived with that beast long enough. I remember the first time he put his hands on me, and you had the gall to say to me, 'One slap is nothing to be crying over.' Well, how about three slaps, or four? How about being punched about the head and face, Mother? How about being stomped? Is that something to cry about? When will it be enough? You tell me, Mother. When should I be allowed to cry? When he has beaten me to death? Huh, Mother?"

"Syreeta, stop—"

"No, Mother," I snap. "I have lived my life pretending that the abuse didn't exist, making excuses for his actions. And now I'm tired. I love my husband, and I love you. But I will not allow either of you to make me accept blame for something I am not responsible for."

Mother exhales in an exasperated huff. "You foolish girl," she says. "I raised you better than this. You're gonna end up with nothing behind your silliness."

"It's too late. I already have nothing."

"Nonsense!" she exclaims. "What on earth are you talking about?"

"Mother!" I snap. "Haven't you heard a word I've said? No, of course not! You only hear what you want. And you're going to believe, and think, and feel what you want no matter what I say, no matter what happens to me. So just do me a favor. Unless you can offer me some words of wisdom, unless you can be objective, supportive and nonjudgmental, I'd appreciate it if you didn't call me." My call-waiting beep sounds. I look at my caller ID and roll my eyes. It's Randy. He has no regard for the judge's order. I don't click over. "Mother," I say firmly. "I don't mean to sound disrespectful, but I am not a little girl. I'm a grown woman. And it's time you start treating me as such. Whatever happens between Randy and me is my business. And whatever I choose to do, I'm the one who has to live with the consequences. Not you."

"Are you going to come to your senses, and let your husband back into his home? The kids need both their parents in the home."

"At what price, Mother? I've turned the other cheek more times than I can count and I've gotten nothing in return except verbal attacks, black eyes, and bruises."

"So now you're going to make your children suffer because you feel slighted?"

"Slighted?" I repeat indignantly. "Are you listening to yourself, Mother, huh? Do you really hear what you're saying to your daughter? You'd rather I take Randy back and allow him to continue to beat and abuse me until he finally kills me, is that it? You'd rather my sons witness their father beating on their mother?"

"Of course not," she says. "I just think you're being irrational. That man loves you. He misses his sons. He has been crying all night and hasn't had a lick of sleep. He's really sorry for what he's done. I think you should be a little more forgiving."

"Mother, I've been crying for almost eight years. Being sorry isn't enough. I want nothing more than to have my husband home—"

"Then stop pushing his buttons."

"Mother, I'm done. Once again, you have proven there's no talking to you. Good-bye." I am hysterical, sobbing uncontrollably. I disconnect her call pushing down on the button, then immediately push it again to dial Dr. Curtis's number. I can't wait until my next appointment. I need to see him now. I am relieved when he says he can see me this evening. After my appointment is confirmed, I call the sitter, then place the phone in its cradle, turning the ringer off.

I blow my nose and wipe my face. When my crying subsides, I return to my sitting room. I sit on my chaise, curl my legs underneath me, then reopen my journal.

Who Am I?

I am flesh and bone, peeking into the womb of the unknown with a heart that beats and bleeds for truths that cling from the breasts of a world that leaks, and sags from the weight of pain and misery.

I am flesh and bone, exploring my identity, looking into the corners of my own mind; seeking answers to a reality buried beneath cobwebs of circumstance; struggling to find a voice that screams at the top of its lungs and makes no excuses for my existence or uses words that flow from the lips of fear or self-hatred.

I am flesh and bone that grows, and breaks, and heals, and breathes in an unrelenting determination to not become my own worst enemy. I am flesh and bone. I am flesh and bone. I am flesh and bone. Covered by scrapes and bruises.

I am flesh and bone created from a past, molded by a present, remembering my pain. Remembering my losses. Remembering my hopes. Still seeking the grace and courage to not just exist; but to live, and to forgive, and ride the wings of love and one day become more than a memory.

When I am done, I shut my book and lay my head back. *Victory begins with me. Victory begins with me. Victory begins with me*, I repeat in my head. I close my eyes and pray.

Nineteen

I enter Dr. Curtis's office wearing neatly applied makeup to cover the bruises on my face. My black eye is hidden behind large designer frames. Dr. Curtis is already sitting, and watches me as I walk toward him to take my seat across from him. He knows before I open my mouth, before I remove my shades, that my beloved husband has beaten me—again. He must have heard it in my voice when I called for my appointment. His eyes are full of concern. I remove my glasses, and he allows me to pour my heart out uninterrupted, reliving and revealing the painful details of the past few days.

"Where were your sons when the police arrived?" Dr. Curtis asks when I finally finish.

"They were still asleep, thank God," I say, letting out a sigh. "There's no way I'd ever want them to witness something like that. Seeing their father in handcuffs." I am not sure why I decided against telling him what K'wan and Kyle had seen out of their bedroom windows that night. No, no. I *do* know why I don't tell him…because I am too embarrassed and ashamed.

"But what about what they've witnessed in the past?"

"Randy has never hit me in front of the children. That's one thing I can honestly say. They've never seen that side of their father."

"They've heard it?" I'm not sure if what he says is meant as a question or a statement, but I answer the best way I can.

"I'm sure they've heard some things. Not a lot, though. Randy usually waits until we're alone, when he thinks no one else will see the man he becomes when he feels provoked."

"But they've heard enough to put them at greater risk for becoming abusers than children who haven't been subjected to violence. The impact of living in an abusive home affects everyone in some way, shape, or form. Your sons, particularly the older two, are more aware of what's going on than you'd like to believe."

What Dr. Curtis says pierces me. He pushes me into a corner, smears this reality in my face. How can I ever give my sons what they need the most—to be protected—when I'm unable to protect myself?

"So what happens now?" Dr. Curtis asks.

I let out an exasperated breath. "I don't know," I say. "There's a part of me that wants to take him back, let him back into our home. Then there's that part of me that wants to let him go before something tragic happens. I am hurt and angry. I can't continue to allow him to abuse me. The next time, he might kill me." My face becomes wet with tears. I reach for the box of Kleenex on the table, pull several sheets out, then wipe my face and blow my nose.

"Although that may not be his intention, the possibility is very real," Dr. Curtis offers. "However, what he does intend to do is create fear whether real or imagined. When he abuses you, he intends to injure you or gain compliance through force and/or intimidation. As you've heard many times before, your husband's abuse is a choice. It is a conscious decision that he has made. So the abuse, no matter to what degree, is always intentional. It is not accidental, and it does not happen by chance."

I allow his words to linger in the air before taking it all in. I know what he says is true. But accepting it hurts. Facing it hurts. And doing something about it frightens me. "What worries me the most is that I have five children, no job, no money, nothing. What will become of me and my sons if I try to do this on my own?"

"I don't have the answer to that," he says. "But what will become of you if you stay, and do nothing?"

I shrug my shoulders. "I don't know. But the scary thing is I'm more afraid of being without him than I am of what he could possibly do to me."

"Syreeta, my job is to give you information, to help you explore options, to process your decisions, and help you develop a safety plan for you and your children. That doesn't necessarily mean leaving. But it does mean being able to be safe. There are no easy answers. Every day is a choice. Whatever you decide comes with a set of consequences."

I take a deep breath. Hold my face in my hands. "I am so confused. Do you think I'm crazy for still wanting him?" I ask, looking up at him. Tears rim my eyes.

"No. You're not crazy. What you're feeling is very natural. You and your husband have a history together. Whether good, bad, or indifferent, you still love him. Your love for him is not the problem. His actions are. Respect for each other's emotional, mental, spiritual, and physical safety and growth isn't an option in a healthy relationship; it is a requirement. I will say this, staying in your marriage, as you know it, has its rewards, and its risks."

I nod knowingly. If I stay, I maintain the lifestyle Randy has afforded me. However, if I stay, and nothing changes, I remain a victim. My tears fall unchecked. "How do you love someone who has hurt you?" I ask this more to myself than to Dr. Curtis. Still, I look to him for the answer.

"With caution," he says.

"What should I do? I need you to help me, Doctor Curtis."

"As much as I'd like to, I can't tell you what to do," he says. "Ultimately, the final decision has to be yours. But I'll be here to help you work it through every step of the way."

I offer him a smile, grateful to have him in my life. "Thank you," I say.

He smiles back. "The journey is just beginning," he states. "It's time you prepare to get to where you need to be, one step at a time. Starting with becoming marketable so that you can become self-sufficient."

"I wouldn't know where to begin," I say. Randy's voice haunts me. *There's no need for you to work. You don't have any skills. And no one's gonna want to hire you, anyway.* Sadly, I believed him. "I've never held a job," I say solemnly. Hearing that truth makes me feel like a failure.

"Managing your home and taking care of your family are both important jobs. But now it is time to be able to earn a living so that you can be better equipped to take care of your sons if leaving ever becomes an option. The Department of Community Affairs offers a program for women who have been financially dependent on the income of another person. It provides employment counseling, job training, placement, and other supportive services." Dr. Curtis hands me a card with the number of the Displaced Homemakers program for Bergen County.

I take it, study the number, then stick it inside my handbag.
I feel as if he has just offered me a lifeline. I pull in a deep breath,
then slowly blow it out. At last, I see a tiny flicker of hope at
the end of a very long tunnel.

Twenty

I am in this world, but I do not exist. I am not living. But I am not dead. I know I am breathing, but I do not feel alive. I am unseen and unheard. Only I see the scars, and hear the screams. Only I feel the pain. Who will believe I have been robbed of my identity? Who will understand that I am afraid? My existence, my purpose, is unknown to me. I am unknown to me. I am empty. And I am unknown to this world, to this shell I am in. But I am here. Yet invisible. And now I have to wonder; did I choose this existence, this way of being, or did this existence choose me?

❖❖❖

I am trying to make sense out of what has transpired over the last few weeks. Yet no matter how hard I try, there is still no logical reason, no sane explanation for why anyone would abuse someone they claim to love. How can anyone get pleasure out of treating someone they claim to adore like a second-class citizen?

I think of all the times Randy made me feel like I was one pill short of losing my mind, anytime I attempted to disagree with him or confront him on anything. How he'd roll his eyes at me, or flat out tell me I was paranoid and delusional; that I was allowing my imagination to run wild and would end up having a nervous breakdown. I think of all the times Randy would call me throughout the day, barking out orders, making demands on my life. How he expected me to carry my cell phone at all times when I wasn't home, and answer it by the third ring. How he thought he owned me. How he kept me on an emotional rollercoaster. How he has made me doubt myself: made me believe everything he said I was, everything I wasn't. How he has enslaved me with his cruel, cutting words. How he has had a commanding power over me that I have not been able to explain.

I reflect on all of Randy's chaotic emotions and realize finally that I am not the one who is damaged. He is. I am not the one who is paranoid or delusional. He is. I am not the one struggling with internal demons. He is. I consider this. I believe this. Still, I get no emotional consolation from this.

Randy invades my mind. He clutters my heart with feelings that confuse me. I struggle to sort through all that he has done, all that I have allowed him to do. I wonder if he is the least bit fazed by what has happened to us as a result of his actions. I wonder if it has changed him in ways that it has changed me. I don't think so. And then I wonder if he feels any remorse. Does he hate himself for what he has done? How does he look at himself in the mirror, knowing that he beat, bruised, and was willing to kill, me? I want to ask him all these questions. I need clarity. I need understanding. I want answers that I am sure he will never be able to honestly give.

Despite the no-contact order imposed on him, Randy calls the house and cell phones. I refuse to answer. He leaves messages that I delete. I will not listen to any of his empty promises. I do

not want to hear his apologies, or his cacophony of sweet noth-
ings that play in my ear like a rickety old violin. He will need
to sit without answers just as I am. He will need to wrestle
with his own conscience for tearing his family apart. I will not
make it easy for him.

Tomorrow I will go to court. I will see my husband for the first
time in almost three days, and I am nervous. I hope and pray
that I will be able to face him without revealing my anxiety.

The phone rings and for a moment, I think it is Randy again.
A part of me, the part that still beats and breathes and depends
on him, the part of me that is blinded by love, hopes it is. In
my state of uncertainty, I am thankful when it isn't. It is my
mother, wanting to know if I have come to my senses, if I am
going to allow Randy back into *his* home.

"Mother," I say. "I haven't given it much thought." I tell her
this although it is far from the truth. It has occupied the corners
of my mind. It is the only thing I can think about. Yet my mind
is engaged in what-ifs. What if Randy comes home and nothing
has changed? What if he abuses me again? What if my sons
become a witness to his abuse? What if he kills me the next time?
What if the police refuse to help me because I've let him back in?

"What do you mean you haven't given it much thought? Don't
you have court tomorrow?"

"Mother," I reply, becoming increasingly annoyed, "I'm sure
you've spoken to Randy so why are you calling me asking me
things you already know?"

"You can mind your snippy tone, Miss Lady. I am still your
mother."

"You're right," I reply. "But that doesn't give you the right to
call here interrogating me."

"I'm doing no such thing," she huffs. "I'm just calling because I am concerned, that's all."

I force a laugh. "Concerned for whom?"

"For you, of course," she states indignantly. "What kind of question is that? You're my daughter."

"Then act like it, Mother. The only person you have ever been concerned about when it comes to me is Randy. After everything he has done to me, you still think he's so great. Well, tell me, Mother. Will your darling Randall be so wonderful when he kills me?"

"Syreeta, listen to you," she snaps. Absurdity filters through her voice. "You are sounding foolish. That man would never do anything like that."

"How do you know that, Mother? What makes you so certain that he wouldn't?"

"Because..." She hesitates, grasping for something that makes sense. "Because he loves you." She believes her answer is enough. It isn't, though. Not this time.

"And he beats me."

"He's promised he would never do it again. It was a bad mistake. He's sorry. He's done nothing but cry. It breaks my heart. He is all torn up over this. Randall is really a good man, Syreeta."

"Well, if you believe that," I say, "then how about you take him back. Because unless you can give me some guarantees that he'll never put his hands on me again, I am not making any promises, and I'm not looking for any. No amount of tears can change that. Bottom line, no matter what I decide, the choice will be mine. And right at this moment, I am not sure what I want to do."

"I don't know what has gotten into you lately. Your tone with me has been utterly unacceptable."

"Mother," I say, pulling in a deep breath, then releasing it. "I don't mean to sound disrespectful. But like I said before, you need to stay out of my marital affairs."

"Is this what that high-priced doctor of yours has you doing? Talking to me any kind of way? You didn't start having these problems until you started going to see that dreadful man."

"That is not true," I reply defensively. "The problems have always been here. I just didn't want to see them. Going to therapy has helped me to open my eyes and see things for what they really are."

She does not hear me. Her mind is made up. "Randall's place is at home with his family. Do you want to become another statistic? Divorced, and a single parent. Do you want to end up living on welfare, or in some godforsaken one-bedroom shack?"

"Mother," I snap. "I'm already a statistic. The first time Randy hit me, I became one."

Her voice grows soft. "He made a mistake," she offers. "He needs you. A man's place is with his family."

I am shaking my head. She is relentless. I realize there is no reasoning with her. I wonder who's crazier, her for believing what she says, or me for wanting to. "Good night, Mother," I say, disconnecting her from my space.

❖❖❖

It is one a.m., and sleep has still not found me. I am tossing and turning, wrestling with thoughts that I have allowed to consume me. No matter how hard I try to close my eyes and push them away, they push back. Becoming vivid sketches of what my life has become. I subconsciously reach for Randy. He is not here. But I am. I am here, alone. I am here, empty. I am here, hurt. I am here, perplexed. I am here, needing direction. I am here, afraid of what may or may not happen.

I get up and check on my sons, then head downstairs to the kitchen for a glass of cranberry juice. I return to my sitting room, watch TV, flipping channels. Despite having over a hundred channels, nothing appeals to me. I turn the TV off, then get up and retrieve my journal, hoping writing will be the elixir I need to doze off. I sink into my chaise, pull my leg beneath me, then begin.

Why, Randy? Why couldn't you love me, and respect me, not treat me like property? Why couldn't you encourage me, allow me to be my own person? Why was it so important for you to beat me, belittle me, and keep me under your thumb? You profess your love for me, but how can this be love? How can wanting to possess and dominate and stifle another human being be love? How can I still love you, and want you, and think about you, after everything you have done to me? How can I find my voice, and still hold on to my feelings for you without compromising myself any more than I already have? Will staying and allowing you back into my space hinder my desire to become my own woman? Will I ever forgive you? Will I ever forgive me?

Tonight I cannot sleep. Tonight I am haunted by you. Your shadow is on my heart. Your existence etched in my memory. I am lonely. And I am missing you. But I do not miss the insults you've hurled at me. I do not miss the pain you have caused me. I want to leave yesterday behind me, but how can I when I can't get through the night? How can I get to tomorrow, when I am stuck in today? How can I say it's over when you cling to my every thought?

I love you, Randy. Despite everything, my heart still aches for you. The very thought of you renders me helpless. No matter how hard I try, I cannot get you out of my mind. But, I refuse to go on pretending that I am happy. I will no longer live a lie. I know that this feeling of emptiness will eventually disappear. And I will heal. I will rise. I will stand. I will survive. I have to.

I admit I am confused and full of contradictions. And I am struggling not to hide behind my neatly constructed mask anymore, the one you still wear. You cannot have me, Randy, until you remove it. I do not want you until you get rid of it. I will pray tonight for you and for me. And tomorrow I will step out on faith. Whatever decision I make will be one I am prepared to live with because I need to do what is best for me, if for no other reason than that. I owe it to myself. I deserve a chance to find myself, a chance to claim my own happiness.

Twenty One

I am at Family Court. The judge asks if I want to file for a restraining order. I say no. He studies my bruised face, tries to see behind my shades. I lift my sunglasses and place them on top of my head, giving him what he wants—a clear view. The judge's eyes narrow as he takes in the blackened mark around my eye, the swelling on the side of my face. He asks if I am certain, wants to know if I have been coerced or threatened in any way. I say *no*. He lifts the no-contact order, but tells me I can come back anytime if I change my mind. He looks Randy in the face and tells him that if he ever comes into his courtroom again on a domestic violence charge, he will try him, and if he's found guilty, will sentence him to serve the maximum jail term. He asks Randy if he understands. Randy nods. The judge orders him to pay a five-hundred-dollar fine and to seek anger-management counseling. *It's not about anger,* I hear in my head. I politely ask the judge if he can go to a domestic violence program instead. The judge tells me it's the same thing. I know it's not, and want to argue that it isn't. I lower my head. I am not ready for Randy to return home. Not with anger management. I look into my husband's eyes and tell him this. Sadness covers his face. He is heartbroken. I am heartbroken also, but for a different reason.

I walk out of the courtroom. Randy is hot on my trail. He calls out for me. I stop, turn around, and face him. He tries to hug me. I step away from his embrace.

"Don't do this to us," he says pleadingly. "The last few days have been hell for me."

"Then you should be able to imagine what it's been like for me over the years, walking on eggshells, wondering when you're going to go off. You have turned our home into a battlefield and I am scared that the next time, I may end up a casualty. I can't risk that."

"Don't talk like that. You make me sound like a monster."

"That's what you've become," I say.

"I'm sorry," he offers. He stares into my eyes. Never flinches. There's pain in his eyes that pierces my heart, causes me to tremble. He reaches for me. I allow him to grab hold of my hands. He brings them up to his lips and kisses them. "I need you so bad," he says softly. "I need my family back."

"I need time," I say, swallowing hard, fighting back the wave of tears crashing against my spirit.

"What about my kids? I need to see them."

"What about them?" I reply. "I would never keep you from *our* sons. I know how much they mean to you. I just don't feel safe under the same roof with you."

"How can you say that?" he asks. "I would never do anything to hurt you."

"But you have, Randy," I say sorrowfully. "Every time you threaten me, every time you beat me or belittle me, you hurt me. That's not the kind of life I want. I don't deserve it, and our sons don't deserve to bear witness to it."

His eyes fill with tears. "Don't you know how much I love

you? I'd do anything to take back what I've done. I'm sorry, baby, really."

"Then prove it," I say. "If you really mean what you say, then prove it. Not with words, but with actions."

"Just let me come home. I'll make it up to you. I've been under a lot of stress, and I'm sorry for taking it out on you. It's just that sometimes you—"

I stare at him, realizing nothing changes until something changes. "No," I state firmly, putting my finger up to stop him. Tears gather in the corners of my eyes. "I love you, Randy, and I want you home more than anything. But this is not about me. It's about you. Until you get help, until you take responsibility for what you have done, our marriage is not going to work."

"I do take responsibility."

I shake my head. "No, you don't. You're saying you do because it's what you think I want to hear. You will say whatever is convenient for you."

"That's not true."

"According to whom?" I ask.

"Don't do this," he says.

"Do what?" I ask.

"You can't keep me from coming back into my own home and expect me to keep paying the bills," he says, trying to shift the conversation. Randy is masterful at diverting attention onto something or someone else.

I stare at him. Allow a pregnant pause to swell as I take in every gesture, every word, as evidence that he is still trying to be in control. He wants to navigate this journey on his own terms. I suddenly recall him telling me on more than one occasion,

"As long as I pay the bills, you don't have a choice. You will do what I say in my house. End of discussion."

"You're right. I can't. But if you want me to go back into that courtroom and ask the judge for a restraining order, I will. I don't want to do that, Randy. We've shared too much. But if you force my hand, I promise you I will. And either way, you'd still have to pay the bills in *your* house. End of discussion."

He grits his teeth and glares at me. I can see in his eyes that he is trying hard to think before he speaks. He is scrambling for resolution, trying to find a way to change his reality. He rubs the side of his head as if he has just been hit with a brick. "So you want me to live somewhere else?"

I nod my head. "For now," I say softly.

He shifts his eyes, looks over my shoulder, then scans the corridor. He bites his lower lip, clenches and unclenches his hands, then palms the back of his head, attempting to squeeze away his frustration. He takes another glance around the courthouse. "For how long?" he finally asks.

How long, I think. I hadn't given that much thought. Time is relative, but extremely important. I am trembling inside, holding back tears. I know if I allow him back home too soon, I will never get out of this vicious cycle. But if I make him wait too long, there may be no turning back. My eyes find his. I steady my voice. "For as long as it takes," I reply. "If you want me, and our family, then you need to prove it."

"How?"

"Randy," I say. "You'll need to be the one to figure it out. But, however you do it, do it because it's what you know you need to do. Not for me, not for our sons. But for you."

"I'll do whatever you want." What he says sounds scripted

and desperate. His words are empty. It is another promise being made without merit.

"No, Randy. This isn't about whatever I want. Because if it were I wouldn't be standing here in the corridor of a courthouse, looking at my husband with tears in my eyes. I wouldn't be afraid to have you home. I wouldn't be feeling torn between holding on and trying to let go. I wouldn't feel empty inside, or feel lost. So...no, this isn't about whatever I want. It never has been."

"Don't say that— "

"Don't say what, Randy, the truth? Well, this is my reality. This is how I feel."

"Haven't I given you everything?"

"Randy, you've given me everything and nothing at all. Yes, you have been a great provider. You've afforded our sons and me a wonderful life. I won't deny that. But not once in our marriage did you allow me to do something for me. Not once have you asked me what I wanted for myself, or encouraged me to do something outside of being your wife and the mother to our children. Everything that I am, everything that I've been, has been for you. And I don't blame you for that. I blame myself for allowing it to happen."

He is silent. I stand there, staring, wondering where this road will lead us. No matter how hard I fight it, I am connected to him. I see a man with a heavy heart, pained and unsure about the direction his life is taking. I see myself in his eyes. I reach for my husband, stroke his cheek with gentle fingers, the kind of touch a woman can only give to a man she loves and understands. He moves his body closer to mine. In that second he allows me to peek into his soul, and I see the man who captured my heart. With tears in my eyes, I repeat my vows in my head, *I will love you in sickness and in health, for richer or poorer, for better or worse, 'til death do us part.* I close my eyes to squeeze away the yelling, screaming, and name-calling. I shut them to blink away the black eyes and bruises. I want to honor my pledge to stand by my husband. I want to hold on to my marriage. But the memories are too overwhelming. Something inside of me feels different. I am changing. This realization frightens and excites me.

In my husband's eyes, I see my past and present. I know that he loves me. And I love him. But, not enough to live in fear, not enough to spend another day hiding and pretending that everything is wonderful. Whatever the future holds is clouded by ambiguity. However, today is clear: I will not allow him to abuse me. I will not allow my sons to be affected by his violence. I can't. I won't. *Every day is a choice.*

"Can I at least spend time with my sons?"

"Tomorrow at six," I offer, breaking away from his gaze.

"You're actually going to give me an appointment to see my own children?"

"You created this, Randy. Being home with your family is a privilege, not a right. If you want your family, you'll need to earn us back."

"Underneath it all," he says, trying to reassure me, "you do know how much I love you."

I don't answer. I look at him one last time before walking out the glass doors, down the stairs, and toward the parking lot. Head high, shoulders straight, stilettos clicking against the pavement, I wrap my arms around my chest, carry the weight of my feelings against my heart, and take slow, steady breaths. When I'm safely within the confines of my truck, I let go of my emotions, break down, and cry.

Twenty Two

Damn you, Randy! I tried to be everything you wanted me to be; everything you thought I should be. And it still wasn't enough. Over and over, I ask the same questions: What did I do to deserve this? Why couldn't you just love me for who I was instead of changing and rearranging me? I've given you every piece of me, willingly and against my will. Still, you couldn't appreciate anything I did. No matter how hard I tried to please you, you always had to demand more of me, had to have expectations of me that I struggled to fulfill. Damn you for hurting me and disrespecting me, and me for allowing you to have this kind of control over me. Damn you for making me feel my self-worth was contingent on you. Damn you for being the cause of my tears. You created this pain. My heart has been bruised. You've hurt my soul. Become the source of my suffering. And I've allowed you to do this to me.

The day slips into an evening filled with an emptiness that has taken up unwanted space, not only within the rooms of this enormous house, but inside the corners of my heart as well. Loneliness assaults my soul, causing the heaviness of tears to rim my eyes. I wonder if I'll be able to stand the solitude. Will I survive the changes that are slowly taking root in my life?

The phone rings for the tenth time tonight. Each time I have refused to answer. However, the buzzing of my cell phone prompts me to pick up. "Hello," I finally answer.

"Syreeta?" Janie asks, letting out a sigh of relief. "Thank goodness. I have been sick with worry."

"I'm fine," I offer.

"Are you really?"

"As best as I can be."

"I guess you know Mother called me."

"I figured she would," I say, plopping down on the sofa.

"How long has he been beating on you?" she asks, cutting to the chase. There is a sharp edge in her tone that I hadn't noticed before now.

I don't feel the need to keep the secret any longer. "For a couple of years," I admit.

"A couple of years," she repeats, disgust coursing through her voice. "Why didn't you ever say anything?"

"Because I didn't want anyone to know. Because I didn't think you'd understand," I say honestly.

Her tone softens. "Oh, sweetheart," she says. "If nothing else, I could have at least been a support to you. I may not know what it's like to be in an abusive marriage, but I do know how to be a friend, and a sister."

"I know you do. I just didn't want you to look down on me."

"Don't you know I love you, and would never judge you?"

I want her to know that keeping my family together has been important to me. That having a happy, successful marriage is what I have believed would validate me. That Randy, and this life, and this love, have become everything. I don't want to be viewed as a failure. "It's too embarrassing to talk about. Letting you know what was going on in my life would have forced me to admit my own truths. That my marriage and my life aren't all I have pretended it to be."

"Syreeta, no one's life is perfect. No marriage comes without compromises and conflicts. But with respect, and love, and understanding, you work things through. People just tend to see what they are most comfortable seeing. Doesn't mean that what they see is what it is. It's just their perception, and their reality. I want you to pack your things and get out of that house. You and the boys can stay here for as long as you need to."

"Thank you," I say, touched by the offer. "But I couldn't impose. You have your own family—"

"Nonsense," she says, cutting me off. "*You* and the boys are my family, too. Our home is always open to you."

"I really appreciate that," I say. "But I need to handle this in my own way, on my own terms. I don't want to uproot my sons. Burdening you and your family with my troubles is not going to change what I need to do. I have to face this head on."

"You don't have to stay permanently. Just come for a while."

"The boys only have another month or so left of school," I point out.

"Then come as soon as they are finished. I'll make all the reservations."

"Janie," I say. "I can't. I don't want to leave my home, or disrupt my sons' lives."

"You won't be disrupting their lives, you'll be taking a break from life up there. It'll give you a moment to think, and us a chance to spend some time together."

"I don't want to drag you into my mess."

"You're not dragging me into anything. You're my sister. And

I love you, and I'm worried about you and my nephews up there all alone."

"We'll be fine." I say this, hoping there is truth in my words. Although I am here without family support, the idea of imposing on my sister and her family makes me uncomfortable. What's happening in my marriage, and in my life, is my mess, not hers. I can't, and I won't, bring my drama in to her life.

"Please, Syreeta," Janie pleads. I can hear the love and concern she has for me in her voice. "Just fly down for a few days. Mother can sit with the boys while you and I make a mad dash south of the border somewhere, anywhere. One week, two weeks, three...who cares? It's my treat. You have to get away."

I chuckle despite myself. "As much as I appreciate the offer, I really can't. I have a lot of things that I need to take care of here. Besides, Kyle and K'wan will be going off to camp for two weeks right after the Fourth of July." I know my excuses are as weak as they sound, but they keep me from telling her the truth. That I do not want to leave my home, that despite all that has happened I still miss Randy. I need, want, to feel his presence which still hovers over me throughout this house.

"Then I'm catching a flight up there first thing tomorrow."

"That's not necessary," I say.

"Yes it is. I don't want you going through this by yourself. Hold on for a minute." She covers the mouthpiece of her phone. I try to make out what she is saying, but every word is muffled. "Sorry about that...You are my flesh and blood, and if Randy has hurt you, then he has hurt me. I need to be there with you, for you. Rodney is online now booking my reservation. I'll see you tomorrow afternoon." She says this before I can try to convince her that I'll be okay, that I can do this by myself. But somehow I know I can't. And she is aware of this.

Twenty Three

Sitting here with my sister comforts me. For the first time in my life, I share my secrets and shame with someone other than Dr. Curtis. My confession frees me. Tears surface around the rim of my eyes. "He had me pinned up against the shower wall, threatened me, forced himself inside of me. Then the next day, he smiled and played the loving husband and son-in-law as if nothing had ever happened the night before. But the minute we got home and the kids were in bed, he shut our bedroom door and backhanded me. Punched and slapped me. Knocked me to the floor, then kicked and stomped on me. He choked me. I actually saw my life flash before my eyes; I knew he'd kill me. It scared me. And I knew I had to do something this time."

"That fucking monster," Janie hisses. "I am so sorry you've had to go through this madness. You need to leave him. Pack up everything and get far away from him," she says with pleading eyes, reaching over and grabbing my hand. "You can't stay here. You don't deserve to be abused or mistreated. You can do bad all by yourself. You don't need him to bring you down."

Leave him? I think. *Then what?* Bring me down? How much further down can I possibly go? I am already at the lowest point of my life. I shake my head. "I can't leave. It's just not that easy."

"Of course it's not. But the longer you stay, the harder it's going to be. You've got to get out now while you can, before it's too late."

"And go where? This is just as much my home as it is his."

"You know you can always come live with Rodney and me for as long as you need, until you can get back on your feet. We have more than enough room."

"And what do I do then? Move my troubles and my worries, and all of my fears in on you and your family? Am I supposed to work for minimum wage somewhere?"

"You can go back to school. Rodney and I know a lot of people. I'm sure one of us can get you a job."

I shake my head. "I appreciate that. Really. But I don't want any handouts. I'm not running from this. If I am ever going to make it out of this, I have to stay. I have to face my husband, and my choices. Whatever changes I make in my life from this point forward are going to be based on what's best for me, not on what someone else thinks I should do, or what they want me to do."

She nods understandingly. She forces a slight smile, yet her eyes betray her. She wants to say more. She wants me to give her an understanding, and answers I myself do not have. I am glad she does not press the issue. "So... Now what? Has he come to the house?"

I look away briefly, nodding. Then I return my attention to her. "He came by this morning to get some of his things," I say, gauging Janie's reaction. There is none, and I do not know if I should be relieved or disappointed. Seeing Randy walk through our home today filled me with so many emotions. Guilt, anger, resentment, and love were all wrapped up in my heart. Watching him move about our bedroom, packing up pieces of his life, flooded me with a hurt that rendered me paralyzed. I stood unable to move or speak as I tried to blink away the realization that our marriage was in serious trouble. But it stubbornly stared back at me, stayed rooted, and forced me to look, and see it for what it was—the aftermath of things gone wrong. When he got into his car and drove away, my spirit shook and caused tears to fill my eyes. Randy had moved out. And I did nothing to stop him. Reliving the moment causes an aching in my heart. "It seems so final," I finally say, wiping my eyes.

She reaches for my hand, then gently squeezes it.

I let out an exaggerated laugh. "You know, Mother wants me to let Randy come back home."

"Is that what you want?" Janie asks.

I don't answer. I look away.

I know without her saying it. I see it in her eyes. *Why?* It is the nagging question I have asked myself a thousand times. It is the same question for which I still have no answer.

"I know you love him, Syreeta," she offers. "But being beaten on, or talked down to, isn't what love is about. Randy has crossed the line."

I know all of this. Believe this. Still...I can't let go. "Yes, he has," I say. "And if I let him back in, it's going to be on my terms. It will be my choice and my choice alone. Not his. Not Mother's. Not anyone's but mine."

She nods again, then she gets up and wraps her arms around me. "I love you. I'll always be here for you."

"I know you will," I say, allowing tears to streak my face. "I love you, too." *And I love my husband.* As I sit wrapped in my sister's embrace, the tears explode from my eyes, and I sob uncontrollably. How could he do this to me? How could he hurt me like this? Why? Why? Why? With each tear shed, there's still no logical answer.

When I am able to pull myself together, I decide to go upstairs, retreat to a long hot bath, then lie down. Janie says she will look after the boys. She gives me another hug, then watches me ascend the stairs. I enter my room weak, weary and teary-eyed. I glance at my unmade bed, sheets rumpled and pillows tossed about like my emotions. I feel like giving up. At this moment, I just want to fall down on my knees, roll myself up into a ball and become lost. Suicide doesn't enter my mind, but disappearing does; going to a place where there is no pain does; becoming invisible does. *And what will become of my sons?* I think as I wipe my tears with the back of my hand. The mere thought of their innocence being robbed from them causes me to bawl. I am aware that this isn't just about me; I have sons who depend on me, sons who need me. *Help me Father. Help me find the strength to get through this.*

I don't know how or when it happened, but I realize I am standing in the middle of Randy's walk-in closet. My hands are sweeping through his neatly starched shirts, pulling them up to my face. I slowly pull in a deep breath in search of my husband's scent. I desperately need to smell his presence. Need to feel him against my skin. I remove my clothes, strip down to the nude, then pull a white dress shirt from its hanger and slip it on. I walk out of his closet, stagger over to my bed, then crawl in, sobbing until sleep embraces me.

❖❖❖

It is six p.m. when the doorbell chimes. I know who it is without checking, but I look through the peephole anyway. Seeing Randy standing on the other side of our door, waiting to be let in because I have changed the locks and the alarm code to our home, shatters all hopes of a happily-ever-after. My reality has come into clear view. There is nothing magical about this moment. Seeing my husband's unshaven face, and weary eyes shakes and crushes what's left of my battered spirit. He has become a visitor in his own home, a temporary guest. I take a deep breath, then unlock and open the door, stepping back and inviting him in. He crosses the threshold and closes the door behind him.

"Hello," he says, stepping into my space. His eyes sweep around the room as if seeing it for the first time, then lock on me. An awkward silence fills the room. There is no doubt that I love him, but he has hurt me. I am still wounded. And I am uncertain if I'll ever heal. He attempts to reach for me but I step away. I know I am still too weak to allow his embrace. I am thankful that, for the moment, I am all cried out.

"The boys are downstairs," I say, moving to the other side of the room, putting enough distance between us.

His stare is intense. "Why'd you change the locks?" he asks. There's a hint of attitude in his voice, but he manages to keep it in check.

I shrug. Swallow the cotton that begins to expand in my throat. "To feel safe."

"From what? Me?"

I look at him, say nothing.

"Why are you doing this?" he asks, slowly moving toward me. "I am your husband. Not some criminal. Not a stranger." I back away, holding up the cordless phone, prepared to speed dial the police. He stops, then steps back and runs his hand over his face. "You're really afraid of me, aren't you?"

"I don't know you, Randy," I say. "I'm afraid of who you've become. And I'm afraid of who I've become. I'm helpless and weak because I've allowed you to have that kind of power over me. I don't want to be that person anymore. Until I can feel safe, until I can trust that you'll never hurt me, or disrespect me again, I will continue to keep my distance."

"I don't want to hurt you. I love you, Syreeta. Right now my only focus is getting my family back."

I shake my head. "No, Randy. Right now, spending time with your sons should be your only focus, and getting some help."

"I don't need any—" He stops himself. "I don't want to be away from you and the kids. I want my life back, with you and our sons. This is my...our home, Syreeta. Our sons need to have both of their parents in their lives, under the same roof."

He knows my beliefs about family, and raising children together as one. But if I am to set an example for my sons of how a woman should be treated, then I can't sacrifice their chances to be better men by staying in an abusive situation. Nothing good can come out of it. I don't want my mistakes to become theirs. "Randy, our sons need two emotionally and mentally healthy parents. They need a father who teaches them respectful behavior toward women, not a man who uses their mother as a punching bag or doormat. They need to see both parents being able to resolve conflicts without the use of violence. And they need to have a mother who's not going to settle, not tolerate, not accept, or make excuses for abuse or disrespect."

"You're right. I'm so sorry for every hurtful thing I've ever said or done to you. I just need you to believe me, and let me prove to you that I'm a changed man." Randy is standing in front of me saying this in a voice dipped in sadness. I try not to take in his scent. Try not to allow him to crawl back into that space in my heart that aches and burns for him, to fill it up with empty promises. I hold my breath because, right at this very moment, it hurts to breathe in his words.

"Have you called the Alternatives to Abuse program?"

His answer is in his eyes. He shifts his weight. "Not yet," he says.

I hear Dr. Curtis's voice in my ear. *Nothing changes until something changes.*

I swallow. Step away from him. "The boys are downstairs," I say, leaving him standing in the middle of the room.

When Randy finally comes up with the triplets in his massive arms, Janie and I are in the kitchen. They are giggling and have become animated chatterboxes, sharing their stories through the eyes of three-year-olds. He puts them down, but they reach up on their tippy toes with outstretched arms wanting to be in his arms again. They miss him. He picks them up and smothers them with kisses. It is clear that he misses them as well. The scene pinches my heart. He sees me staring at him. There's a pleading in his eyes. He allows me to see him holding our babies; allows me to hear their joy and see their smiles. He knows what this will do to me. When he puts them down, he plays with them a while longer and engulfs them with more hugs before sending them back downstairs. He walks toward the kitchen entrance, then stops in his tracks when he realizes there's someone else in the room.

"Hello, Janie," he says, surprised to see her. He walks over to give her a kiss, but Janie scowls. She abruptly gets up from her seat and slaps my husband's face, her nails grazing his cheek. He is staggered. I am shocked. She has forgotten that my children are downstairs. I have never seen this side of her.

"If you ever put your hands on my sister again," she spews, venom dripping from her lips, "I will personally put you out of your misery."

Janie is rooted in place, ready to strike him again. Her nose is flared; there's a fire in her eyes that frightens me. I gently touch her arm and give her a pleading look in an attempt to extinguish the flames before they spread into a wildfire. She glares at him, then reluctantly goes downstairs to check on the boys, leaving us alone.

Randy touches his face. There is blood on his fingertips. He looks at them. I grab a towel, wet it, then hand it to him. "I guess I deserved that," he says, holding the cold towel to his cheek.

I don't say one way or the other if he does or doesn't. I don't acknowledge the pain in his eyes, the hurt that matches the unnerving aching in my chest. He created this. He did this to us. I will not wear the blame. I will not shed any tears for him, not this time.

Twenty Four

As the days drag into weeks, this separation becomes less painful and the tears are less frequent. Today is over. Sunset has come and gone. With the exception of the light from a full moon, the sky is dark. I have the gas lamps and outdoor fireplace lit. For the middle of June, it is unseasonably cool tonight. Randy has taken all of the children. This is the first time he will have the triplets for the weekend. I try not to worry. Try to believe he can manage. I convince myself that I am not needed. Still, I find myself stealing peeks at the phone, waiting for it to ring. It doesn't.

Janie and I are outside on the deck, sitting and sipping on chilled glasses of Chardonnay. We have just stepped out of the Jacuzzi and are lounging in matching bathrobes. Our heads are wrapped in big towels. Donny Hathaway is floating around us from the Bose sound system. Janie's three-week stay has been a godsend. Our relationship has changed. There's a closeness that we never shared before. Secrets and laughter and tears have sealed our bond. I am going to hate to see her leave, don't want this new connection gone. She has given me something special. Something I will always cherish. The gift of sisterhood.

Without Janie here, I know Randy would have been back home already. He'd be back in our bed. Back in the emotional space I am trying to sort and clean out. And I would be caught once again in the spokes of his unpredictability, spinning helplessly around in circles.

Though I am relieved by his temporary absence, there are those nights when I still reach over in bed, wanting to feel him next to me. Needing to lay my head on his chest and listen to the beat of his heart. There are nights when my body aches for him. He is the only man I've loved. The only man I have ever been intimate with. In my head, I know I don't, never did, deserve how he has treated me. But in my heart, I am hurting. He is all I know. What did I do to deserve this emptiness? I am an emotional mess. How will I ever make it without him?

"Do you miss him?" Janie asks, cutting into my thoughts. Her eyes are on me.

"Every day," I admit, taking a slow sip from my glass. "But it's not as unbearable as it was the first few days."

"Do you still want your marriage?" Janie questions. "Because if not, I have a soror who practices law in Jersey and New York that I can refer you to. She's a high-powered attorney who will get you everything you deserve. When she's finished, you'll walk away a very wealthy woman. Trust me. Randy will pay for all of your pain and suffering."

I glance around my expansive manicured yard, take in its beautiful landscaping, then pull in a deep breath. I am not ready for a divorce. Nor do I want to make Randy pay for anything. I want him to get help. Change his behavior. Not for me, but for himself. I want him to be a better man, a better father. I am aware of my feelings for my husband, and I know reconciliation is a possibility. Its likelihood is as real as the sun, bright and blazing. I blink back my truth, the burning realization that I will most likely take my husband back. However, *when* becomes the ever-changing question.

I nod my head, then place my face into the palms of my hands, confused and dizzy from my own uncertainty. "Yes, I want my marriage. But I want peace of mind more," I say, looking over at her. "And unless Randy is willing and able to change…" I pause, afraid to speak my words into existence. There is still that part of me that clings to hope with everything I have. I don't want to go on with life without him. I'm not ready to cross that bridge. But the reality is what it is. "If Randy is incapable of loving me, if he is still invested in trying to control me, and abuse me, then it will be over between us. It will have to be." I say this with a conviction that surprises me. Unfortunately, I am not certain just how much truth it holds.

She looks at me, concern glittering her eyes. She reaches over and takes my hand, squeezing it. I smile. She smiles. We both drift off, without saying another word, wondering.

Twenty Five

"I left him once," I blurt out.

"Who?" Dr. Curtis asks.

"Randy," I explain, leaning back in my seat. Almost eight years ago, with a toddler and six-month-old infant in tow, I packed my bags and walked out on Randy. There wasn't one particular thing that he had done for me to leave him. I suppose it was an accumulation of things. I was feeling overwhelmed and neglected by him, and was tired of his constant ridicule. Nothing I did was ever right. Everything that didn't go right was my fault. His constant putdowns were wearing me down. I just got sick and tired of being sick and tired. So I woke up one day, and just up and left him without any thought.

I got in my car with only two thousand dollars in cash and one credit card, and drove off. I knew if I went to my mother's or sister's Randy would find me, so I went to Maryland to stay with a good friend who lived there. She said I could stay with her for as long as I wanted. She told me not to worry about anything, that I would be safe with her. But somehow Randy tracked us down, and ended up at her doorstep, ringing her bell. He banged on the door, making a scene. She wanted to call the police, but I begged her not to, and against her advice I went outside to calm him. At first he begged me to come home.

Then it became a demand, filled with desperation. He told me I had no business trying to take his children away from him. That I was going to ruin my sons' lives by leaving. When I still refused, he stepped up to me, leaned into my ear, then whispered, "You either get your ass home, or I will burn this bitch's house down with you and her in it." His eyes were bloodshot. His face was demonic. I had never seen that look in his eyes before and it frightened me. His threat seemed real. I was more afraid of what he might do to her, than to me. She didn't deserve to be hurt or dragged into my problems. So I gathered my things and returned. He made it very clear that if I ever tried to leave him again, he'd hunt me down and kill me. I believed him, and was too afraid to find out whether he'd carry out his threat.

"How long were you gone?"

"Two months," I reply. "But I wasn't strong enough to stay gone. I went back because I had to. I was afraid of what he might do to me or my friend. Besides, the pressure of having two small children, and the fear of raising them alone with no other place to go was unbearable." I shake my head. "I had no other choice. So I went back to him. Things were good for a while, then gradually returned to what I had tried so hard to get away from. I feel so stupid."

"Why?"

"Because," I say, feeling torn, "I went back when I shouldn't have. But at the time I really believed it was the right thing to do. I believed it was the only thing I could do."

"You are far from stupid," Dr. Curtis reassures me. "Your reasons for going back are yours. The blame isn't. You don't have to try to explain why you did what you did. As I've stated many times before, staying or leaving isn't the issue. Domestic violence is a widespread problem. Women who stay in abusive situations, or return to them, have their reasons. It's definitely not always because they want to, but because they sometimes feel they have to. Out of guilt, out of love, out of loyalty, out of fear, out of confusion, out of societal and familial expectations many women are forced to make the difficult decision to stay, or return. And many women fear that no one will believe them if they reveal or report the abuse.

"Sadly, abusers force their victims to stay by destroying all other options. They alienate you from family and friends and make you emotionally dependent on the abuser. They aren't violent all the time and will often do and say things to remind you of why you fell in love with them in the first place. As I mentioned in another session, research shows that most women who attempt to leave their abusive situations will return to the abuser approximately eight to nine times before they finally leave for good."

I feel a knot coiling in my stomach. All through my marriage, Randy has had me believing that I could never make it without him, and that I would be nothing without him. That no one would want a woman with a bunch of children. That I was damaged, used goods. It has taken all of this for me to realize, to believe, something different. That I am somebody, that I am worthy of loving and having someone love me back, not controlling me. Not dictating my life. Not choosing my thoughts and feelings, but, allowing me to be myself, allowing me enough room to grow. I honestly know if I am to break this cycle, if I am to live by example, if I am to teach my sons to respect and honor women, I cannot and I will not return to Randy, the man who has beaten and disrespected me, the man who stripped me of my thoughts, my feelings, and my own choices. I will not go back to that existence.

I have never stood up for myself. All of my life I have tried to keep peace. Tried to keep everyone happy, never wanting to disappoint anyone. Not my mother, not Randy. Growing up, I did everything asked of me, never spoke back to my parents. I always tried to be the perfect daughter. And now in my marriage...it's been the same thing. I have tried to be the perfect wife and mother; tried to keep everyone happy. But no matter what I have done, or have tried to do, somehow it has never been enough. At the end of the day, I have been the one blind to the truth: that I can't please everyone; that I can't make everyone happy all of the time, no matter how much I may want to. And it's okay.

My thoughts slip back to when it all began. It was a few months after my first miscarriage. Randy and I were having Sunday dinner over his parents' house when his mother stated how sorry she was that I'd lost the baby. "Maybe the next time she'll get it right. Otherwise I might have to find someone else who can," Randy said. His remark, biting and cold, startled his mother and punctured me, but Randy laughed and pretended he was only joking. That's how it began, with one putdown. Gradually, I became entangled in his web. His words became his weapon— mixtures of sharp, blunt, hot, cold, jagged, and piercing expressions of his frustrations, disappointments, and dislikes.

Slowly, it escalated to ridiculing, name-calling, cursing, screaming, and blaming me for any and everything that went wrong. His sporadic tirades about my cooking, my cleaning, about my appearance, about the way I cared for our children became emotionally draining. Nothing I did was ever good enough. I didn't understand what was happening, didn't realize I had been caught in a trap of domestic violence. Didn't know I was stuck in a cycle. Didn't believe it would happen to me. You don't comprehend that you have been mentally ambushed until you are deeply wounded and scarred. Until you sink so far down in a pit that you can't see your way out. Until guilt and shame has your soul chained. So I learned to pretend it wasn't happening to me. Pretend that my marriage was perfect. Pretend that things would get better. Pretend that I could make it through another day.

"How will I know he's changed?" I ask, still hoping I can save my marriage.

Dr. Curtis leans back in his seat, considers my question. He knows the purpose of my query. I am still holding on to hope; still embracing the possibility of reunification.

"You'll know he's changed when he is no longer violent or threatening to you; when he can acknowledge that his abusive behavior is unacceptable and wrong; when he takes full responsibility for his behaviors, no longer blames you, and understands he does not have the right to control you or try to dominate you; when he respects your right to say no, and respects your opinion even if he doesn't agree with it; when you no longer are afraid of him or feel intimidated. Then and only then will you see change."

"Sounds like he has a long way to go," I state solemnly.

"Real change doesn't occur overnight," he offers.

I nod, knowing Randy's journey is not mine. We have come to a fork in the road, and the direction he takes is solely up to him.

I go home, ask the sitter to stay a few hours longer, then retreat to my sitting room and open my journal. Other than my sessions with Dr. Curtis, writing is the one thing that soothes me.

Silence of the Heart

I listen
And hear
The nothingness
That lingers deep
In the corners
Of my soul;
Soft whispers that blow in the wind
And slip into the dawn of my dreams
And become rainbows of my fears.

I watch
And I see
Memories tossed in the air like confetti
Slowly falling
Disappearing
Piece by piece
Into the pit of my own emptiness;

I touch
And I feel
A loneliness that runs through my veins
And constricts
The pulse of a heart
That no longer beats
Because there is no you
And there is no me

Twenty Six

It is eleven o'clock at night. Randy is outside, ringing the doorbell. I pull my bathrobe tight around my waist, then go to the door, asking him what it is he wants. "Randy, what are you doing here?" He is wearing a baseball cap, gray sweats, and a Morehouse T-shirt. His eyes are red and swollen. His face is unshaven.

"I've been trying to reach you all day. Where have you been?"

He still feels the need to question me. I think for a second. Is he asking out of concern or out of his need to control me?

"I was out," I reply.

"All day?" he asks.

I decide I will not allow him to continue his inquisition. "Randy, you still haven't answered my question. Why are you here?"

"I want to come home," he says softly. There is demand in his eyes, and desperation. "I miss you. I can't live like this. Let me in so we can talk, please."

Although what he asks of me sounds more like an order than a request, his tone is pleading. I want to tell him no. Tell him to come back another time, at a more decent hour. But I don't have the heart to turn him away. Don't have the nerve to close the door in his face. Reluctantly, I step aside, let him in. "Only for a minute," I say.

"I can't believe you're treating me like a stranger. This is still my home, too."

"Would you rather the kids and I move out, and let you move back in? If you want this house, Randy, you can have it. A house without love is nothing but a structure, not a home."

"Yes…I mean, no." He takes a deep breath. "I don't want you to go anywhere. I don't want to go anywhere. I want my family back."

"You can't have us back. Not until you can guarantee me you will never disrespect me or put your hands on me again. Not until you can treat me like a partner instead of your prisoner. I am your wife, not your slave. Until you can realize that, until you can accept that I am entitled to have my own mind, my own opinions, and make my own decisions, being with your family is not an option."

His eyes offer me no such assurances. We both know this. His voice grows soft, tenderness and hurt rolled up into a ball. "I never thought this is how our life would end up. I never thought you'd want to walk away from everything we have."

I cringe. He is still trying to make this my doing. I will not allow him to suck me into his funnel of guilt. "I didn't ask for this, Randy," I say gently. "I never imagined this is where we'd end up either. But we have. Where we go from here will depend on you. I'm not walking away from what we've shared, because there have been good times. I'm walking away from being abused, and leaving behind the woman who was afraid to stand up to you."

"Is there someone else?"

It takes a moment for what he has asked to register. I blink, blink again. *Oh my God*, I realize. *He thinks I am having an affair.*

If only life were so simple. I almost want to laugh at his ludicrous question. I dare not tell him that after all I've been through with him that I don't have the strength, energy, or desire to be with anyone else. That there is nothing left of me to give.

His intense stare is unsettling. "Are you saying you want a divorce?"

I haven't thought that far. Do not want to see that as an option, not yet. "No, I'm not saying that. I mean, I still want to believe there's a chance for us. But right now I need time to digest everything that has happened between us. I need time to heal."

His eyes pull away from me. His voice is low, but heavy from the weight of his feelings. He is hurting. I am hurting. "I love you. I am so damn lost without you and my sons. I miss you, Syreeta. Being away from you and our sons is driving me crazy." He moves closer to me, the heat from his breath caressing my face. He reaches for my hand. "I don't ever want to hurt you again. And I don't want to lose my family." His eyes glisten with tears. "I know I've screwed up big time. I'm realizing that now. I'm gonna do whatever I have to do to fix this. I promise I'll make it right. Just don't give up on me, on us."

"I don't want to," I say, backing away in order to put a safe distance between us. My knees are wobbling. At this very moment, I don't know if it is him I fear, or me. Although he has said or done nothing to warrant concern, I am still scared that he'll hurt me. I reach into my robe's pocket to make sure I have my cell phone. I hold on to it, glancing over at the cordless phone resting on the coffee table. My eyes scan the room for safety zones. Just in case.

Randy notices. I wonder if he is aware of the safety plan in my head. "I'm not here to hurt you, Syreeta," he says, reassuring me. "Being arrested, seeing the neighbors' lights go on, and having to go to court to stand before a judge was the most embarrassing and humiliating thing I've ever had to go through. And now I'm without my family."

Despite myself, I feel his shame. I empathize with him. Luckily, I do not feel the need to apologize for something he causes. This is a bed he has made, one he must lie in. *Maybe getting arrested is what he needed*, I think. "I wish…I mean…I don't want to live with resentment toward you. I don't want to harbor any hate."

"You hate me?" His question sounds like a statement dipped in pain. I do not want to lie to him. I have to give him the truth the best way I know how.

"I don't want to, Randy," I answer. "I am trying so hard not to. But I—"

"Do you still love me…miss me?"

"What does that have to do with anything? It doesn't change what has happened between us."

"Answer my question," Randy challenges. He is asking for a lifeline, one I can easily refuse him, but won't.

"Yes," I say.

He sighs. Relief, hope, and opportunity are in his gaze. "Let me stay the night," he says. His eyes bore into mine. "I wanna spend the night in our bed, holding you in my arms. I need you, Syreeta."

I dare to look at him. In that split second, he peers into my heart and allows me to see into his. I can't deny it. There is still a connection that runs as deep and wide as the Atlantic Ocean. He is my husband. I am his wife. We stare at each other. I am not sure what I want from him or from myself at the moment.

He is sure of what he wants from me, certain that it will reseal the edges of our lives. Despite the yearning that stirs and finds its way to the center of my heart, I am unable to share his sentiments. I do not want to confuse or complicate things any more than they already are.

I wonder if Randy can hear my heart pounding through my chest. Wonder if he knows. Wonder if he can sense that I am vulnerable. He closes the space between us. Pulls me into his arms, begins kissing me. He kisses my eyelids and gently strokes my face. His tongue finds its way into my mouth. He grinds himself into me. Runs his fingers along the small of my back; his hands are opening gates I am trying to shut. I begin to feel the heat. A fire ignites. I try to contain it before it spreads through me. I do not want to give mixed signals.

Say it. Stand up to him. "No," I say, pulling away from him. "I can't do this."

He is surprised that I am refusing him. "No," he repeats, reaching for me. I try to step away from him, but he grabs me by the arm, yanks me toward him. "I am still your husband." He realizes what he has just done and lets me go.

"What's next, Randy? Are you gonna hit me now?"

"No," he offers hastily, trying to reassure me. "I'm...um, look, baby. I'm trying to change. I know the way I've treated you over the years hasn't been right. I don't ever want to treat you like that again. But I can't change overnight. I need you, baby, to understand that it's not gonna be easy for me. And you have to accept that there may be times when I show that side of me. It doesn't mean I don't want to stop it. It just—"

I stare at him, trying to wrap my mind around what he is saying. But I cannot and will not. "No, Randy," I reply firmly.

"I don't have to accept it and I won't. The next time you put your hands on me, there won't be a no-contact order or restraining order. It'll be a divorce. And I mean that." After the words come out of my mouth, I realize that I will not be able to retract this, that I will have to stand by what I've just said if I am ever to be taken seriously.

He raises his hands in surrender. Steps back. "I'm sorry," he says. "I didn't mean to grab you."

"That's the problem, Randy," I point out, rubbing the print he has left on my arm. "You never mean to do anything you do to me."

"You know that's not true. I don't mean to hurt you."

"But you do. And you have. And I'm tired of it."

"Don't do this to us, please. I didn't come here to argue."

"You did this to us, Randy. So please leave before I call the police." I pull out my cell, gripping it in my hand.

His eyes bore into mine. He is wounded. I am not sure if he's preparing to attack or retreat. And I will not wait to find out. I flip open my cell, ready to push the preprogrammed number for the police. He does not argue, frown, or try to change my mind. Instead, he hangs his head, draws in a breath, then heads toward the door. He stops, turns back to face me. A tear glides down his face.

His voice is just above a whisper. "I love you."

I say nothing. There are a new set of rules being written. Rules that I am comfortable accepting in my life, that I can live with. Rules he will need to learn to respect. I watch my husband walk out, slowly closing the door, leaving behind the echo of his words.

Twenty Seven

It is now the middle of July. Almost two months have gone by, and Randy and I are still living apart. He has found himself a condo in Fort Lee. He pays the household expenses here and deposits money into an account every two weeks for me and our sons. I am not sure if his guilt compels him to be so giving, or if he truly does accept responsibility for what he has done. Maybe it's a mixture of both. However, he says he will continue to make sure we are taken care of, no matter what the outcome between us. He says I am the mother of his children, his wife, and no matter what I think about him, he would never want to see me out on the streets. He tells me that he is willing to give me all the space I need. That he knows he messed up and may lose me. That he never meant to take me for granted. He cries when he says all of this. And I go to him, pull him in to me, embrace him in a way that is new, and very different. Yet, I do this knowing and feeling that I am not the same woman. That my perceptions of him, and me, and our relationship are changing.

My cell phone rings. I recognize Randy's number and pick up. "Hello."

"Hey," he says. "How are you?"

"I'm making it, one day at a time," I say. It does not feel like he is my husband and I am his wife. We are certainly drifting. I'm not sure in what direction, or if this nomadic experience will bring us back closer together. The tones in our voices have become formal. We have become estranged and strangers all at once. I am not clear in my heart or mind what I am supposed to feel or not feel about it.

"Me too," he replies. I can tell he wants to say more. I allow him the room to do so, but he chooses not to, and I am okay with that. "Listen, I was just calling to let you know I have to work late tonight so I won't get a chance to stop by to see the boys."

"I appreciate the call. I'll make sure to let them know."

"I'll call the house, later, and speak to them before they go to bed, if that's okay with you."

"That's fine," I reply. "You can call them anytime you want." I say this and mean it. He is their father, and I will never interfere with his relationship with them. I will never use them as pawns to get back at him for the turmoil he has brought into my life. This strain, this divide in our marriage, is between Randy and me.

"Also, I'll be picking the boys up a little earlier on Friday. Like, around four."

"I'll make sure they're ready."

"Okay, thanks. Talk to you later."

"'Bye," I say, disconnecting the call.

I am happy he is not taking his frustration at our separation out on our sons. Pleased that he is trying to rebuild and maintain a relationship with them. Three nights a week he comes by to spend time with them. He takes the two oldest boys on every weekend, and every other weekend he takes all of the boys.

K'wan is still distant. Kyle struggles with his allegiance to his brother and his desire to protect me. He rides the fence. He loves me, and loves his father. I don't want him to ever have to choose. He never has to. I tell him this. Tell K'wan this. Reassure them both that I love them just as much as their father does; that we will both be in their lives, no matter what happens between Randy and me. We will always be their parents.

I am thankful Randy is no longer badgering me, trying to manipulate his way back home. That I don't have to drag him into court for child support, or worry about allowing him visitation with his children. That he is being civil and trying to treat me like an equal instead of a subordinate. He is four weeks into his Alternatives to Abuse group. I am hoping he is getting something out of it. He tries to convince me that he has changed. I don't believe he has. I'll admit he no longer tries to blame me for our separation. He tries to accept some responsibility. Some isn't enough, but it's a start. Still, it does not seem as if he internalizes any of what he says. I recognize he's just stopped his behavior until he gets what he wants. Until I give in. However, as far as I'm concerned, he has twenty-two more weeks in counseling to go before I consider taking him back. I love him, and am painfully aware that I always will. We have a history together. We are connected through our experiences and there are some memories I want to hold on to. Others, I am trying desperately to put behind me.

There was a time when I felt and believed I needed Randy to feel complete. Needed him to assure, and reassure me, that I was important, and worthy. But, now when I look at him, I don't yearn for his approval. Don't seek his validation. Don't need him to complete me. I am not half a person. I am a whole person with flaws who has hopes, and dreams, and visions. He can either accept me as I am, or not. I am learning to accept that life goes on. People move on. They grow apart. And that every day is a choice.

This new reality is refreshing. It is what inspires me to get up this morning, drop the triplets off at day care, go to my hair salon, and cut my hair off. Not completely, but it is still a dramatic change. It now hovers slightly above my shoulders with a hint of honey-streaked highlights. Gone are the days of flowing hair to the center of my back. Hair I was forced to grow and keep because it was what Randy wanted, what he desired.

On my way home, I stop at Mangos of New Jersey in Hackensack and order dinner. I am done with starving myself to maintain a weight that Randy deems acceptable. I will eat smothered turkey wings, yams, and cabbage, then eat a slice, or two, of coconut cake, and savor every mouthwatering forkful. I am no longer Randy's life-sized Barbie doll. I am Syreeta Taylor. Yes, wife and mother. But, more importantly, I am Syreeta Colette Taylor—a woman learning to make her own decisions.

Twenty Eight

I arrive at Dr. Curtis's office fifteen minutes before my two p.m. appointment. His receptionist, Carla, greets me, tells me she will let him know I am here. I thank her, then sit down. India.Arie's "Beautiful" is playing. I have heard the song before, but today I am really hearing the words for the first time. I smile. Hum along. Yes, I want a place known as beautiful. Dr. Curtis buzzes Carla's line and tells her he is ready to see me. She informs me of this. I smile and make my way toward his door.

He greets me as I walk in. "Hello," I say, making my way across the room. Today he is sitting behind his desk. I take my seat in front of him.

"How have you been?" Dr. Curtis asks.

"I'm doing well."

"How are you sleeping?"

I shift in my seat. "Not too badly," I offer.

His eyes are on me, studying me. He accepts my answer. "Have you heard back from the Homemakers Program, yet?"

"Yes," I say. "I have an appointment to meet with one of the counselors next week."

He smiles. "That's good news. I'm really glad to hear that. And how are you feeling about all of this?"

"Good, I mean, excited," I reply. "This will be the first time that I'm doing something for myself." I tell him I have decided to take the ten-week computer course that is offered. Tell him they will help me with my resume and help me find a job when I am done. I thank him again for the referral.

"No problem. I'm just happy you called. How are your sons doing?"

"They're adjusting," I say. "K'wan and Kyle are more affected by this than the triplets. They are still too young to really understand what has happened between me and their father. But I am worried about K'wan and Kyle. I don't know what I will say to them when they start asking questions. What am I supposed to tell them?"

"That the violence is not their fault," Dr. Curtis says. "That it's not right to hurt other people. Let them know that getting angry does not mean it's okay to hit someone. That there are better, healthier ways to solve problems. Let them know how much you love them."

"Do you think I should say something to them about all of this?" I ask.

"I'd encourage you to let them talk if and when they are ready to. Be ready to listen to them and acknowledge their feelings. If by some chance you start to notice a shift in their behaviors, you may need to take them to counseling to help them sort out their feelings and fears."

"I want to do whatever it takes to help them get through this; so that we all can heal from this."

He nods knowingly. "That's the best thing you can do," he offers. A pregnant pause fills the room before Dr. Curtis continues. "And Randy? How are the two of you getting along?"

"He hasn't tried to kill me," I say half-jokingly, "if that's what you're asking me."

"Well, not exactly. But that's a good thing to know," Dr. Curtis says.

I realize after I say it that this isn't a joking matter, and that I shouldn't make light of it. "I think Randy believes I am going to take him back and be the same woman I was."

"Do you believe you're the same woman?"

I shake my head adamantly. "No. I'm definitely not."

"Do you believe Randy is the same person?"

"I'm not sure. I think it's too early to tell. I mean, I can see that he is trying. I want to believe that he wants to stop his abusive behavior, but I also realize—thanks to you—that stopping a behavior doesn't necessarily mean he's changed."

"Exactly," he concurs. "Change doesn't happen overnight. It will take a lot of work on his part." He pauses, opening his arms. "So tell me. What do you believe is different about you?"

I think about his question, consider my answer, then look him dead in the eyes. "I am more aware," I say with certainty. "I understand the dynamics of domestic violence, and how easy it is to get caught up in its cycle. I have learned that being informed allows a person to make better decisions, something I am now learning to do. I don't ever want to fall back in that trap. I am aware that I have to keep working on myself to make sure that doesn't happen. Now that I have finally found my voice, I don't want to lose it. Because I know that at any time I can end up right back in the same situation, either with Randy or with someone else down the road. You know, Doc, I owe you so much."

He looks at me surprised. "How so?" he asks.

"You have helped me to see a lot about myself, and my marriage in the short time I've been coming to see you. I am convinced that it was part of my fate to bump into you that day at the mall, and for you to hand me your card. I know it was divine intervention. There's just one thing."

"What's that?"

"How did you know? I mean, how could you tell I was a victim of abuse?"

"I couldn't. There was just this dark cloud hovering over you that told me you were maybe not a victim of abuse, but definitely a victim of circumstance, a victim of forced choices. Sometimes we are forced to do things out of fear, or because we can't see beyond what life is already offering us."

Forced choices, I repeat in my head. There is something about what he says that rings true. Tears surface in my eyes. I dab at them, preventing any from falling. "I know I still have a lot of work to do. But coming here has made me feel so much better. It's like a ton of bricks has been lifted off my shoulders. I understand, I mean really understand, that there are always choices in every situation. We all have them. But sometimes they seem too difficult to make because they can come with life-altering consequences, changes that we may not be ready or able to handle."

"You're absolutely right," he says, closing my file. He leans forward and props his elbows on his desk. He steeples his fingers beneath his neatly shaved chin. "Every day is a choice. Sometimes we can't see that. Sometimes we don't want to. Other times we're not ready to. But every day we always have access to a new set of options. No matter what, everything a person does—or doesn't do—is a choice."

I nod.

"Are you still writing in your journal?"

"Yes. Any time a thought or feeling comes to me, I write. It's actually been helping me."

"Good," he says. "And have you given any more thought about the support group?"

I nod. "Yes, I have."

"And?"

By leaps and bounds, I have been making remarkable progress. I know I still have a long way to go to get to where I need to be, but I feel confident about the new direction in which I am heading. I now know the more supports I have in place, the easier this road I must travel will be. "I'm ready," I state proudly.

He smiles, approval written all over his face.

Yes, I am more ready than I could ever imagine. I have learned some hard lessons. Lessons that have taught me a lot about who I was, about who I thought I needed to be, and about who I want to become.

Twenty Nine

I am deep in thought, my face wet with tears. I am having good days and bad days, and today is a bad one. I am missing my husband. I am blaming myself when I know I shouldn't. I am struggling with guilt that I know doesn't belong to me. I am lonely. I am second-guessing my decision, wondering if I am doing the right thing. Was I wrong for calling the police? Am I wrong for refusing my husband his family? Am I wrong for going against his belief, and my mother's belief that a man rules the home and a woman never contradicts him, that she is not allowed her own voice? Am I wrong for wanting to become my own person? Am I making this out to be more than it really is? Can I make it without Randy? Do I have to give up on myself in order to love my husband? Today I am overwhelmed with questions. I do not know if I can get through this. Do not know if this is what I really want. Today is definitely my worst day. I gave Randy the best of me, gave him all of my heart. And today I am mad at him. I am mad at myself. I don't want to be. But I am, and I don't know how not to be. I am trying so hard to wrap my mind around what I need to do to get through this. I can't seem to.

My sons' faces flash through my mind, and my tears fall rapidly. Will they blame me for what has happened? Will they grow to hate me? Have I caused them undue pain? These questions constantly invade my thoughts. Like a broken record, they play over and over in my mind. Knowing I don't have the answers causes an unbearable ache. I replay my conversation with K'wan in my head.

"Is Daddy coming back home?" he had asked, sitting on the edge of my bed, his face etched with concern.

I'm not sure exactly how to answer him. Not sure of what he is expecting outside of the truth. I search for an answer. "I don't know," I finally said. "Why? Do you want him to?"

He shakes his head. His face is void of expression. "No," he says flatly.

A part of me is not surprised by his response; still I feel the need to press him for reasons. "Why not?" I asked.

"Because I don't like him."

He is entitled to his feelings; still what he says stings. "That's not a nice thing to say about your father," I said.

He lowers his head, shrugs his shoulders. "He hits you," he replied. "And makes you cry."

I hear Dr. Curtis in my head. *Let them talk about their feelings. ...Show understanding.* I allow K'wan to vent, but still feel the need to defend his father. Still feel the need to protect him. So I make excuses for him. Hide behind my own denial. "Your father doesn't mean to hurt me," I explained. "He doesn't know how to handle his anger when he gets upset." He looks at me disbelievingly. I cringe as the words fall from my mouth. *It is not about anger.* I am torn. I don't want to lie to my son. Don't want him to be misled. He deserves the truth. But I am unsure of how much I should share. *Violence is not the answer.*

"Your father and I have to work on some things before he can come home."

"I hope he never comes back," he stated. I look in his eyes, see pain swimming along the edges. "I heard him yell at you and say nasty, mean things to you. I'm scared he might hurt you really bad. And then we won't have a mommy. I don't want him to hurt you anymore. Can't he just stop hitting you and being mean to you?"

I couldn't run from my son's truth. He had cornered me, forced me to see his pain. He is afraid for me. I am afraid for myself. My eyes filled with tears as I sat and listened to my ten-year-old son articulate his worries. I pulled him into my arms, kissed him on his forehead. He hugged me tightly. "I won't let him," I replied, rocking him in my arms.

He looked up at me, his face wet with tears. "You promise, Mommy?"

"I promise," I said. I held my firstborn close to my heart and silently sobbed.

The knocking on the door pulls me out of my reverie. "Mommy. Telephone."

"Who is it?" I ask, wiping my face with the backs of my hands.

"It's Grandma Ellen," Kyle says, walking in. I am not surprised. I knew it was only a matter of time before she called. Randy speaks to his mother daily and I am sure he has told her everything he wants her to know, everything that keeps the focus off himself. She is the kind of mother that still babies her grown son, struggling to let go—to allow him to be a man. She has always doted over him; he can do no wrong in her eyes. Never has and never will. And this will be no different. Kyle hands me the cordless.

I wait for him to walk out the door, then say hello.

"Syreeta, how are you, dear?"

"I'm doing well, and you?"

"Are you sure everything is all right? I've spoken to Randall and he told me what has happened between the two of you..."

I am not interested in having this conversation. Do not want to hear how much he loves me and his children. How her only child is so wonderful. How well he provides for us. How good he is to me. How much he has sacrificed for us. How I should try to be more understanding. I already have too much on my mind. I don't need or want to be reminded of how my marriage is in shambles. Don't want to feel any worse than I already do. In my head, I hear Dr. Curtis tell me that I am not the problem; that I am not the cause. I hear him saying that sometimes doing the right thing doesn't feel so right; that this guilt is not mine to own. Any other day I believe him. But today...today, I'm not sure what I believe. I brace myself, ready to tell her this when she surprises me with her own confessions, knocking the wind out of me.

"...He told me he is out of the house," she continues. "After all he witnessed growing up, I cannot believe he would lay his hands on you. He saw what his father did to me, and he swore he'd never be like him. But look at him. He turns around and becomes the same man he's fought so hard trying not to be. He knows better. I can't believe all of the nasty things he has said and done to you over the years. I am so disappointed and hurt by what he has told me."

I cannot believe what I am hearing. Can't believe Randy actually admits to putting his hands on me. Can't believe he witnessed his mother go through years of emotional, mental and sometimes physical violence growing up in his home. That he heard his father yelling and screaming and cursing his mother. Saw his mother cry, heard her beg and plead and scream for help. Saw the bruises. Randy's mother shares how her husband expected everything to be just so, in perfect order. How nothing was ever to his satisfaction. How she was afraid to stand up to him, or ask him what his expectations were. I can't believe she tells me how she left him three times, and kept going back. Randy has always painted his childhood as wonderful, led me to believe that his parents had a great marriage, that everything in his life was perfect. I suppose everything was. In his world, the one he created in his head, it had been. But today, his mother pulls the blanket off his lies, revealing all of his secrets, the ones he has masterfully kept hidden from me. The ones that damaged his youth, and shaped him into the insecure man he is. He has tried to keep the truth from me, has kept it from himself. And I am the one who has had to suffer the demons of his childhood.

"Mrs. Taylor," I state, trying to absorb everything. "I had no idea."

"Of course you didn't," she says. "It's not something we ever talked about. When I left his father the last time I vowed to never go back, but he kept tugging at my heart. The memories of what we shared, and the love I had for him, nearly overwhelmed me. But I stood my ground. His father knew I was not going to budge. That he was going to lose his family."

"How long were you gone?" I ask, feeling a connection to her I've never felt before. On some level I was relieved that she could honestly understand my experience because she had gone through it herself.

"The last time I left him, I was gone for almost a year before I decided to go back," she says. "I don't know what happened, but his father decided to change, and he stopped abusing me.

He apologized to Randall and me for everything he ever did to us. I gave him another chance. We cried. We forgave. And we moved on with our life as a family. We decided to put it behind us, and never bring it up again. Randall was thirteen when the fighting finally stopped. There were twelve years of hell in our home before then. It affected Randall and me in many ways, but we overcame. At least I thought we did."

I am at a loss for words. Her admission stumps me. "Mrs. Taylor, I don't know what to say."

"I don't want you to say anything. I just want you to know that I understand what you are going through. That I do not condone what Randall has done. He is my son, and I love him. But this"—she takes a deep breath, then sighs—"putting his hands on and disrespecting you is not acceptable. He's been calling me almost every day crying. I know he is pained, but this is something I cannot fix for him. I told him he needs to get some help before he loses you and his children, if he hasn't already. And to be honest with you, I wouldn't blame you one bit if you decided to not take him back. But know this for certain, he *will* take care of you and my grandsons, no matter what."

Families are a privilege, not a right. Tears gather in my eyes. "Mrs. Taylor," I ask, "why are you telling me all of this now?"

"Because," she says, "you have a right to know. I've always believed you can't hide the truth but for so long. Eventually, it will reveal itself. Randall should have shared this with you. I told him not to keep it from you. But, he said it wasn't important, that there was no need to rehash the past, so I respected his wishes and left it alone. However, deep in my heart, I feared that one day something like this would happen. He is so much like his father. The first time he insulted you years ago, after you lost the baby, I pulled him to the side and told him I never wanted to see or hear that kind of behavior again. And he promised me, he wouldn't let it happen again.

"But obviously, it has gotten progressively worse. I know things are hard right now, and you are probably dealing with a thousand and one different emotions. Whatever you do, please try not to blame yourself for Randall's behavior. Don't beat yourself up, trying to carry guilt that is not yours. My son created this mess. Just know that whatever you decide, I support you one hundred and ten percent. If there is anything you need or anything I can do, please don't hesitate to call me. I want you to know I am here for you. You do not have to go through this alone. I will be on the next plane up there if you need me."

"Thank you, Mrs. Taylor," I say, deeply touched. "I appreciate that. But that won't be necessary."

"Well, you just let me know if and when you need me, and I'm there. I know we are not as close as I would like for us to be. But I want you to know that I love you as if you were my own daughter, and I would really like for us to work on being much closer than we are."

I break down and cry. She is saying the things my own mother has been unable or unwilling to say. She has reached out to me in a way my own mother has failed to do. She is not blaming me. She understands my pain. She knows what it is like to be berated, disregarded, degraded, and oppressed. She reminds me that this is not my fault. This comforts me. Although I feel a tinge of resentment that this is not coming from my own mother, I feel emotionally vindicated.

"That's right, sweetheart," she says soothingly. "Get it out. It's okay. You are a strong, beautiful woman. You will overcome this.

You will survive this. You have to believe that God will see you through this. Yes, he will. Hopefully, my son will realize what he has before it's too late. I am going to keep you, Randall, and my grandsons in my prayers."

"Thank you," I say in between sobs. "Mrs. Taylor, I am so glad you called."

"It was long overdue, sweetheart," she says. "It's something that should have been said years ago. But now you know. What you do with what I have shared is truly up to you. You needed to know. If you need me, call."

"I will."

"I love you."

"I love you, too, Mrs. Taylor."

"I know you do. Give my grandsons big hugs and kisses for me. I hope to visit sometime this summer."

"I will," I say. "That would be nice."

We say our good-byes, then hang up. My mother-in-law's phone call confirms that this wasn't made up in my head, that I didn't imagine this. Her call reinforces what I already know. That I can get through this. That no matter what happens I am going to be okay.

Thirty

I'm not exactly sure when it happens, or how it happens. But, today, as I look in the mirror, I see something different in the reflection staring back at me. My bruises have faded. The black eye is gone. And I can finally see...me. Although the image is familiar, there's something remarkably unfamiliar about the vision before me. I have become a woman slowly collecting the pieces of her life, sorting through her choices, and putting back what she needs while discarding what no longer holds any value in her life. I no longer see guilt, or blame, or excuses magnified in my eyes. With all of my flaws, and mistakes, and frailties, I see acceptance. I see forgiveness. I see new beginnings. I am embracing a new me.

Summer is over, another school year begins, and Randy and I are still trying to find a rhythm that keeps us moving forward. We are still dancing around any discussions of reconciliation, mostly my doing. I am not ready, and Randy knows this. Surprisingly, he doesn't push the issue. He continues his group counseling. I continue my weekly sessions with Dr. Curtis. And I will remain in treatment so that I do not lose my voice. I am so grateful for his presence in my life. He has helped me to help myself, and save myself. He has been my sunshine. No, better than that. Dr. Curtis is my angel, my therapist with wings.

I feel, for the first time in my life, that I can, because I believe. I am, because I believe. I am rising. I am standing. I am recovering. I am surviving. And I am so thankful.

Next week, I will begin the Displaced Homemakers' Office Technology Program. It is a ten-week program that takes place Monday through Friday from 9 a.m. to 4 p.m. Upon completion, I will participate in its job search training program, and hopefully obtain employment. My goal is to one day become self-sufficient. To one day be able to take care of myself and my sons without having to rely on Randy or anyone else. Even if Randy and I do reconcile, I do not want it to be because my back is up against the wall and this is my only option. I want it to be because it's what I truly want for myself. Not because I am trapped, or pressured.

Some may think I am being foolish to consider walking away from everything Randy has afforded me; that I am crazy for wanting to work when I don't really have to. I am not a fool. And I am not crazy. Foolish would be staying and acting as if everything is perfect. Crazy would be expecting things to be different and doing nothing about it. Bottom line, if I want any level of financial independence I do have to work. It is not the pay I am focused on; it is the experience and the chance for opportunity. It is the social stimulation and the sense of freedom I am looking forward to. It is the groundwork for a new foundation for myself.

Tomorrow I will start the domestic violence support group for victims. I am ready to share my experience with others; to hear their pain and finally break my silence in the presence of others. Each week, Dr. Curtis shares more statistics, more news clippings of women being beaten and killed. This confirms what

I have painfully come to understand. I am not the first, nor will I be the last, woman to be abused by a husband or lover. Another life will be taken. Another home will turn into a battle-field and another woman will be savagely beaten about the face, the back, or her pregnant belly. By the hands of her attacker, her flesh will be bruised; by the words of her aggressor, her spirit will be broken. Another soul shattered. I can only pray that somehow, someway, someday, she finds the courage, the inner strength to leave, or at the very least to identify another set of options that keep her safe, before her life is taken; before her children become motherless. I pray. And I pray.

The doorbell rings. Randy is here to pick up the boys and do whatever a father does to bond with his sons. I open the door, invite him in. He smiles, still very handsome to me.

"Hello," he says, closing the door behind him.

"Hello," I say back. The triplets run to him, faces bright. He bends down and scoops them up in his arms.

"How are Daddy's little men doing?" he asks, locking his eyes on me.

They giggle, try to answer in the best way they know how. They are happy to see their father. He basks in their innocence, in their unconditional love for him.

"K'wan, Kyle," I call out. "Your father's here."

I watch them make their way down the stairs, faces painted in uncertainty—boys who are growing, one day becoming men— and I wonder how much of an impact my choices will have on their lives. Try to imagine how the ones I've already made have affected them.

They give me hugs, then greet their father. He greets them back, giving them hugs, embraces they accept with caution. "I want you boys," he says to them, "to take your brothers outside. I'll be out in a minute."

"'Bye, Mom," they say in unison.

"'Bye, sweethearts," I say. They gather their overnight bags, then head out the door.

Randy looks at me, studies me, then smiles. "I like it," he says.

"What?" I ask.

"The hair," he answers. "It makes you look…younger. I almost didn't recognize you when you opened the door."

I return the smile. "Thank you." His stare feels hot on my flesh. But I don't react. I allow him to take in all of me.

"I really thought I made you happy," he says. "That's all I ever wanted to do."

"At one time," I admit, "you did. But the problem is that my happiness should have come from within. I should have made myself happy. Not you."

"I wish you would have told me a long time ago how you felt. Maybe things wouldn't have gotten so out of hand with us."

I know problems, like blisters, do not manifest overnight. It takes a long time for them to emerge, to fill up with unspoken words, half-truths, and misdeeds before they erupt.

"Maybe," I state, "in my own way, I did try. But you weren't ready to hear it. So here we are. I accept my responsibility in this. Although I am not responsible for your abuse, I take full responsibility for my choices. I didn't have to stay. I could have left you a long time ago. I could have stood up to you, called the police on you. But I didn't. I wasn't ready to admit there was a problem in our marriage. The reality is it began and ended with you treating me like you owned me, and me allowing it."

It takes him a while to comprehend what I have just said, but he eventually gets it. He looks at me as if he is finally seeing me through a different set of eyes. "You're not the same," he says.

"You're right," I reply. "I'm not the same woman I was a few months ago, or a few years ago. I'm not even the same woman I was yesterday. Every day I am evolving. I've had to, for me." The woman who lived in fear, who was afraid to gather her voice, who was controlled and being manipulated, is gone. In her place stands me.

He walks over and reaches for me. I allow him to touch the side of my face, then run his fingers through my hair, allow him to touch me in a way I haven't permitted in months. He kisses me lightly on the lips. I pull away. I do not want to cloud my judgment, or do anything I may regret later.

He doesn't react. He respects my boundaries and backs away. He is learning. "I apologize for every unkind thing I have said or done to you. You didn't deserve it. I look at you, and I see what I have done to you, to us, and I am really messed up over it. I know saying I'm sorry doesn't change what's been done. I know you've heard it a thousand times before. But it's something that needs to be said. I will do whatever it takes to make it up to you. I just hope one day you will be able to forgive me."

I am not sure if he will ever be able to make up for all he has done. I'm not even sure if that's what I really want from him. I am working on forgiving him. I know forgiving him will not mean that he has been let off. It just means I am relinquishing his hold on me. It means I am giving myself permission to let go, to heal, and to move on. But I am uncertain where he will fit into my life once I am done finding my way.

"In time," I offer, folding my arms across my chest, "I'm sure I will."

He nods, takes me in for a while longer, then glances at his watch. "I gotta get going. I'm taking the boys to the movies, then out to eat."

"Have fun," I say, opening the door. The boys are outside, running around, playing and laughing, oblivious to the length of time their father and I have been talking.

"Do you have any special plans?" he asks, walking out the door.

I follow behind him, smiling to myself. My life is now full of choices that I can freely make for myself. I can do whatever I want, or do nothing at all. This is still all very new to me. But it excites me. "I haven't decided."

"Maybe we can talk later on this evening, after the kids are asleep."

I hold his gaze. "Maybe," I say.

He smiles. "I am always going to love you, Syreeta. You are engraved in my heart. I'm willing to fight to win you back. No matter how long it takes."

"Every day is a choice," I respond. He looks at me, unsure of what I have just said; as if there is some hidden meaning behind the words. I leave him with his uncertainty. I don't feel the need to elaborate. "Enjoy your weekend," I say, waving at my sons. I watch him walk toward them, then gently close the door. I press my back up against the door, then let out a deep breath.

Something Dr. Curtis once said in a session begins to manifest inside my head, causing a wave of emotions to sweep through me. "Beneath your bruises is a beautiful woman who will heal," he stated. At the time, I heard him but didn't really understand. Back then, I was unable to conceptualize what he had said. Couldn't imagine what that process would feel or look like. Didn't even know how I would begin the journey. But I have, and I am. And I finally got it.

Today, I understand that I am truly the gardener, the cultivator, the master of my own life. It is my responsibility to embrace a new way of thinking, a new way of feeling, a new way of being. Who I am as a woman, is not about Randy, not about my mother. Not about the perceptions of others. Not about their acceptance. It is about me.

As I look out the window, watching Randy load the triplets into his truck, then strap them into their car seats, I smile. Not because of what I see, but because of how I feel—different. In such a short time, I have changed. I am not the same woman I once was. Trapped and scared. Voiceless and confused. Beaten and bruised.

I liken my life—this new journey on which I am embarking—to a puzzle, a thousand pieces with varying shapes and sizes, trying to find their fit one piece at a time. As I sort through my needs and wants, my hopes and dreams, I am carving out a new path for myself, one step at a time. I am piecing together a new life, a new me. And I am embracing change.

I will never deny my feelings for Randy. I love him. He is my husband, and the father of my sons. But I don't love him enough to ever sacrifice my identity again. Not enough to ever lose pieces of my spirit again. Not enough to ever relinquish my power to someone else. Not enough to be reshaped and remolded into someone other than what I need and want to be. Not enough to be defined by (or confined to) the expectations of someone else. I want nothing more than to salvage my marriage, but my priority is saving myself. I am a work in progress. I am learning to become the dancer, and the drummer, of my own life. I have no control over what happened yesterday, and no control over what may come tomorrow. But, today...at this very minute...I have control of what I say, think, feel, believe, and do. And I have the power to make choices that can either hurt or heal me. Add value to my life or hinder it. At any time, I can decide to stand at the edge of the cliff and wait to be pushed over or take a step back to keep myself safe. I know change isn't always easy. And it truly hasn't been. But that's okay, because nothing worthwhile ever comes easy. Every day, I am getting stronger. I am growing, and learning. I am taking back what belongs to me. I am unlocking my chains.

I understand this defining moment, this evolution, this coming into my own, comes with some risks and losses. But the rewards are much greater and hold more meaning. I have found my voice. I am shedding. Peeling back layers of old ways that have kept me weighed down and trapped. And in the process, I am getting back my self-worth.

I have decided that if I allow Randy back into my life, this time he will not get to pick and choose parts of me and discard what doesn't suit him. He will either accept all of me, or have none of me.

Am I afraid? Yes. A part of me is very much afraid of being without my husband. I am aware that if I take him back there is a possibility that his old ways will resurface. But if that does happen the difference this time is I won't allow him to ever pull me back into his funnel of abuse. I cannot allow my love for him to ever cloud my judgment or my ability to protect myself emotionally, mentally, spiritually, or physically. So if nothing changes with him, then divorce is inevitable.

As I open my journal, I think, I remember, I embrace, I create words that sum up where I've been, where my choices have taken me, where I am finally heading. And I cry. Not tears of sorrow, or tears of regret, but tears of hope, and forgiveness, and healing. Bittersweet tears that remind me that it is okay, that I am okay. I smile, wipe my face, then pick up my pen and allow words to flow.

Beneath the Bruises

Black and blue
Purple and red hues
Prints of a hand
Dents from a fist
Slaps
Kicks
Verbal attacks
Cut through the core of her being
And her heart shudders
Against the clutter of words
Harsh and vicious
Hurled like hot fire against her flesh
Burning
Smoldering
Blistering
Instinctively she curls into herself for protection
Helplessly
She lays in mourning
Haunted by the ghosts of abuse
Can you see her tears?
Taste her pain
Hear her deafening silence
Whispering
Pleading

Whimpering
Grieving
Getting lost
Quietly
Unblinkingly
She confronts her reality
Painful
Bittersweet truths
That she loved someone more than they loved her
Trusted someone more than they trusted her
Gave more than what was given
As a token of love
And it hurts
It disappoints
It damages
It destroys
Beneath the bruises
She is tormented by
Maybe if I were...
Maybe if I did...
Maybe if I could...
This uncertainty follows her wherever she goes
Echoes in her mind
Clangs in the emptiness of her soul
Like the beat of heavy drums
Pounding
Thumping
And she pleads for relief
Begs for mercy
And despite herself she forgives

Because it is in her nature
It is what she does
It is who she is
And she weeps
Until her heart aches
Until she has emptied out
And rinsed away
All of her pain
Until she has cried her last tear
  Suddenly something miraculous begins to happen
The marks of violence darken
Then lighten
Then slowly fade
And she begins to make a commitment
To herself
That no one will ever bruise her again
Disrespect her again
Hurt her again
Never again will she lose herself to someone else
And she realizes she is not to blame
She is not accountable
For someone else's insecurities
For someone else's self-hatred
She no longer has to wear this badge of shame
It was not her fault; was never her fault
And it is okay
To be her own woman
To want more for herself
To demand
To expect

To want
Respect
Honesty
Understanding
To hope
To dream
Finally
She becomes responsible for herself
Her own happiness
Her own choices
Her own mistakes
Beneath the bruises
She sheds her skin
Peels back layers of unhealed wounds
Discards the pain
And she learns through her experiences
That she is worthy
Of loving
Of being loved
Being respected
Being valued
Being herself
Beneath the bruises
She rearranges
Regains her dignity
She's a survivor
Deservingly
She lets go of time and space
Surrenders
Moves on

And emerges from her shell
Not seeing life—
Her life
Through the hollow eyes of someone else
But through her own bright lights
Curious and wide
In bursts of vibrant colors
She sees
Reconstructs her existence
Bit by bit she picks up the pieces
Throws out what she no longer needs
Replaces what's been missing
And slowly
The puzzle of her life begins to fit
And she is no longer afraid
No longer fears
There will be no more tears
And she understands her self worth isn't contingent on anyone else
Beneath the bruises
She cocoons herself in her emotions
Hibernates
Hides
Becomes invisible
Raw feelings
Self-doubt
Turns to
Self-love
Self-pity
Turns to
Self-awareness

And she learns no one defines who she is
Or who she will become
She doesn't blame the past
Instead
She falls down on her knees
And
Prays
And prays
And slowly she heals
Begins to mend
Finds the strength from within
To take back what belongs to her; what had been stolen from her
Her dignity
Her self-worth
Her self-respect
Her self-confidence
Her self-esteem
Her sense of direction
And slowly
Methodically
She rises
Beneath the bruises
She finds the key
And
She rises
And unlocks herself
From her prison
And says, "Thank you"
Unshackled
Unchained

Unbound
Unrestricted
Everything becomes crystal clear
And she sees what she hadn't been allowed to see
Reflecting
She feels what she wasn't allowed to feel
And she rises
Moves forward
Finds her passageway
Recollects what she's left along the way
What she's given up
Beneath the bruises
She rises
Reconnects what's been disconnected
Replenishes what's been depleted
Redefines her purpose
Recreates her image
Renews her spirit
Redirects her journey
Reclaims her heart
Beneath the bruises
She rises
Beneath the bruises
She rises
And gives thanks
Beneath the bruises
She rises
And gives praise
As she holds her head up high
Spreads her wings

Expands her horizons
And
Inhales
Deeply
Intently
Breathes in the promise of something beautiful
Holds on to the moment of self-discovery
Exhales
Slowly
Blows out what used to be
Wraps her arms around herself
Lovingly
And
Embraces a new beginning
Today
Tomorrow
She faces the world
Her world
Full of challenges
Full of visions
Full of hope
And
In the bloom of her womanhood
She lives
She breathes
She thinks
She feels
She believes
She knows
She is no one's victim

She's a survivor
And
In her eyes lie
The magic of love
In her smile
The promise of brighter days
In the sway of her hips
The confidence of her beauty
In the curve of her lips
A rainbow forms
And the sweet melody of a happily ever after
Rings loud and clear
She understands love isn't pain
She realizes abuse isn't just physical
That verbal
And emotional
And psychological
And sexual abuse
Cuts deep
And scars as well
And she has decided
There will be no more battlefields
No more assaults on her mind
No more invasions on her spirit
No more attacks on her body
No one will possess her
Or control her
Ever again
She won't compromise her needs
Won't settle for someone else's misdeeds

She shapes her desires
Around her own decisions
Her own situations
Beneath the bruises
She is healing
Beneath the bruises
She is joyful
Prayerful
Thankful
For she's at peace
Finally...
Because she is free

When I am done, I reread what I have written, inhale, then blow out the sweetest sigh of relief. I allow my tears to fall unchecked. Yes, beneath the bruises, I am a woman, healing; a woman, growing; a woman, uncovering; a woman, discovering... me. I am finally giving myself permission to live, and breathe, and be happy. Because, at this moment, I now know exactly what Syreeta wants for Syreeta.

ABOUT *The* AUTHOR

Dywane D. Birch, a graduate of Norfolk State University and Hunter College, is the author of *From My Soul to Yours*, *When Loving You is Wrong*, *Shattered Souls* and *Beneath the Bruises*. He is also a contributing author to the compelling compilation, *Breaking The Cycle* (2005), edited by Zane—a collection of short stories on domestic violence, which won the 2006 NAACP Image Award for outstanding literary fiction; and a contributing author to the anthology *Fantasy* (2007), a collection of erotica short stories. He is the author of the novella *The Goddess of Desire* in Zane's erotica anthology *Another Time, Another Place*.

He has a master's degree in psychology, and is a clinically certified forensic counselor. A former director of an adolescent crisis shelter, he continues to work with adolescents and adult offenders. He currently speaks at local colleges on the issue of domestic violence while working on his fifth novel and a collection of poetry. He divides his free time between New Jersey and Maryland.

You may email the author at bshatteredsouls@cs.com